An Uneasy Truth 2

Lady B

Copyright © 2018 Tamika Jonhson

All rights reserved.

DEDICATION

First and foremost, I wanna give praise to my higher power without whom none of my blessings, supporters or craft would be. "My higher power wouldn't let me quit." -Lady B
To my seedz, my wolfpak I love you beyond measure y'all will forever be my reasons Tamira, Jaieden, Dennis, Z'kai & Lord y'all are my driving force to success. To my love DJ thanx for supporting the movement & keeping me on my toes love u bunchez.
To my Bloodline y'all are everything thanks for the encouragement and endless love. Sista & Twin y'all already know I love u to life I do dis for us we all we got. Uncle you are the best thanks for being all I need in a male role model. To my Chocolate Star and Grandma although you aren't here to experience these milestones with me I feel your presence and strength Imma keep you smiling I love you.
To my lovely editor Yara Kaleemah:Thank You for lighting that fire!! We doing it again baby ROUND 2. Thanks so much for your guidance, dedication and patience with both of my projects (An Uneasy Truth 1 & 2) I luv and. appreciate you my sista in Lit.
To my Cover assassin Dynasty, my models Patricia (Catwalk), Cami Adams and my baby brother Jay (Twin) as well as my many friends, family, supporters, promoters, reading groups, fan clubs etc…THANK YOU, YOU ARE APPRECIATED!
Oh Yeaaaa!!!! & A VERY Special s/o to You! yeah you for picking up this book ENJOY!!
And to everybody else in the words of 2Pac "Can you see me now? Am I clear to you?"

--LADY B

Strong Women Achieving Greatness Presents
An Uneasy Truth 2
Written by: Lady B
Cover Art by: Dynasty's Cover Me
Copyright 2018 by Authoress Lady B

This novel is a complete work of fiction. Any characters and situations mentioned within the content of this novel are figments of the author's imagination. No parts of this novel may be modified or copied without written permission from the copyright holder.

Chapter 1

Summore had been sitting in her car parked a few cars down from Troy's apartment for the past 4 days cooking up her plan to pay Troy back for dissing her. Night had fallen when Troy started to feel a little hungry, so he grabbed his keys then went into his bedroom to check on Sky and Lem who were wrapped up in playing Call of Duty on Xbox 360.

"Y'all hungry?" Troy asked.

"Yup," they both said in unison, never taking their eyes off the television.

"Y'all good staying here while I run around the corner or y'all riding with me?" He asked.

"We good," Sky said as she turned and smiled at Troy. She had begun to get used to Troy and liked him being around.

"Ok cool. Don't open or answer the door no matter what," Troy said as he headed out the door. He called Isis to see if she wanted anything to eat seeing that it was almost time for her to get off.

"Hey beautiful, I'm headed to the carryout you want something…," Troy began saying when he was suddenly struck in his head from behind causing him to drop his phone. He stumbled a few steps trying to shake off the dizziness while attempting to get a look at his attacker when he was struck repeatedly until he was knocked unconscious.

"Hello! Hello! Troy!" Isis yelled when she heard the loud crack and an unfamiliar male voice say something she couldn't make out. She knew for certain that wasn't Troy's voice, something inside her told her this was bad.

Isis grabbed Cita by the arm quickly and pulled her to her side of the party they were doing at a hotel not too far from her apartment.

"What's up Sweetz? Why you all aggressive?" Cita asked with a smile until she looked at her friend's frightened facial expression.

"I gotta go. Something ain't right at home," Isis said as she started to gather her duffle bag, not going into full detail of what she had just heard on the phone. She didn't bother to change out of the long sexy see-thru one piece she had on.

"Okay go ahead baby. Just text me when you find out what's going on," Cita said as she hugged her friend goodbye.

Isis sped thru traffic trying to get home as fast as possible. When she got to her street, it had been blocked off. She parked on the next street, opened her duffle bag and pulled out some clothes she threw on her sweat pants, t-shirt, and sneakers and jogged back down to her street. When she reached her building, an ambulance was speeding off. Standing there in the doorway of her building with an officer, she saw her children in tears then noticed all the blood in the hall.

"Mommy! Mommy! Oh my God..." Sky cried as she rushed into her mother's arms and cried.

"Excuse me ma'am, are these your children?" the lady officer asked in a sympathetic tone.

"Yes. What is going on? Where is Troy?" Isis asked trying to calm the panic inside her heart.

"Mama, it was so much blood. All he wanted to do was go get us something to eat," Lem said in an outburst of tears as he hugged Isis.

"Troy has been rushed to Washington Hospital Center. He's been severely beaten and stabbed. Your daughter is the one who found him. Had it not been for her, he would've been dead on arrival," the officer said before walking away.

Summore sat calm and content with her work. Her only worry was the little girl who saw her run out of the building. She didn't give her actions a second thought as she rode away from Isis' block.

Isis grabbed her kids by the hand and headed to her rental in a hurry.

"Mommy, is Troy going to be ok?" Lem asked with tears in his eyes as they walked back up the block to Isis' car.

"I don't know baby. We're going to the hospital right now," Isis replied as she jumped into the car and sped to Washington Hospital Center. Sky and Lem were both scared because they didn't understand why Troy was attacked. Sky sat trying to process exactly what she saw.

An Uneasy Truth 2

She knew she had to tell her mom who she saw attack Troy but first she needed to see that Troy was ok.

Isis parked in a handicap parking spot and she and her kids ran into the hospital. They frantically hurried to the nurse's station where a heavy set brown skin woman with dimples sat heavily engaged in something on her cell phone.

"Excuse me ma'am, can you please tell me where I can find a patient by the name of Troy Davis?" Isis asked, interrupting the nurse.

"Ok gimme one sec," she replied, never taking her eyes off her cellphone screen.

Isis stood as patiently as she could with her children waiting on information while the nurse continued with whatever had her so attentive to her device.

"EXCUSE ME!!!" Isis yelled, slamming her hand on the counter in front of the nurse, startling her and causing her to give all her attention to the matter at hand.

"What was that name again?" The nurse asked with much attitude as she sat her phone down and began to type Troy's name in the computer. Isis looked down and noticed the nurse's screen was on Candy Crush and that caused her to flip out.

"Troy Davis is his name. But are you fucking kidding me? I'm asking for information on my friend who could be possibly dying and you got me on pause for some fucking Candy Crush! What fucking room is he in?" Isis yelled in the nurse's face. An officer heard the commotion and walked over to see what was going on.

"Ma'am is everything ok?" The officer asked.

"I'm asking this bitch where my folks at in this mu'fucka and she gon put me on fucking pause for some damn Candy Crush like she ain't at fucking work," Isis said angrily as she ushered her children to two seats in the waiting area, they themselves were too worked up as soon as she walked away to continue to address the nurse they followed right behind her.

"Ummm, well you ain't gotta be disrespectful. He's in surgery. I'll send word back so one of the doctors can come speak to you," the nurse said as she popped her gum and rolled her eyes at Isis.

"You young so I'm not even gonna hop over this fucking counter though," Isis said as she walked away, looking for another nurse who could help her with Lem and Sky on her heels. The officer caught up to Isis and assured her that he would have the doctor come see her once they were done. Isis and her kids sat in an isolated nearby waiting room to prevent her from slapping the taste out of the young, unprofessional nurse at the front desk. Four hours later, a small, Asian doctor walked into the waiting room.

"The family of Mr. Troy Davis," she said looking around the waiting room.

"Yes. Right here," Isis said as she laid Sky's sleeping head in Lem's lap and walked out into the hallway with the doctor.

"I'm Dr. Young and I performed your friend's surgery. You are..." Dr. Young asked.

An Uneasy Truth 2

"I'm Isis Monroe. Troy is my friend and neighbor. He was watching my children when this happened. How is he?" Isis asked trying her best to keep the tears that were welling up in her eyes from falling as she rocked from side to side, wringing her fingers.

"Well, Ms. Monroe, your friend is stable for now. However, he was beaten badly and stabbed a half inch from his left renal artery which is a major artery. Had it been hit, he may have died before arriving here. He isn't out of the woods just yet. There's some swelling on his brain so we have him medically sedated," Dr. Young explained.

"Oh my God. Oh my God, how bad is his brain swelling?" Isis said as she began to pace the small hallway.

"Ms. Monroe, honestly, right now it's hard to tell. These types of things can range from mild concussions to severe, permanent brain damage. We'll be monitoring him closely and running a few tests. Please leave your contact information so that you can be reached if there is any change," Dr. Young said as she gave Isis a warm hug and walked away.

"Ok thank you, Dr. Young." Isis said as she wiped away her tears and walked back into the waiting room to get Lem and Sky.

"Is everything okay, ma'am?" The officer from the front desk asked.

"Not really," Isis replied as she struggled to lift Sky from the seat she was asleep on.

"Let me help you with baby girl," he said as he lifted Sky and carried her out to Isis' car.

Isis unlocked her doors so that the officer could put Sky inside. Lem climbed in and buckled his seat belt.

"Thank you so much Officer... Officer Blue," Isis said as she looked at his badge for his name.

"No problem at all. You drive safely," Officer Blue said as he turned to walk away. Isis started the car and rolled her windows down preparing to pull off then she heard a familiar voice from the passenger window.

"Aye, baby girl I ain't mean that shit," Vee said as he grabbed for the door. He had been following her for the past two days just waiting on his moment to pounce. And seeing that Troy wasn't glued to her hip gave him the green light.

Isis began to scream causing the officer to turn quickly and rush back. Vee spotted him as he got closer and pulled out a Glock 40 and started to bust shots. Isis' first instinct was to get her children to safety as she whipped her car out of the parking lot as fast as possible and into traffic, not looking back. Sky awoke screaming from the gun fire that had erupted between Officer Blue and Vee.

Isis looked at her through the rearview mirror and spoke to her daughter as calmly as she could, trying to calm herself and Sky down. Lem hugged his little sister tight as she cried. He too shed a few tears not out of fear, but out of anger. It was anger toward his father whom he had seen on many occasions hurt his mom. Though he never spoke of it, the abuse stayed with him. Isis saw a BP gas station ahead and stopped to comfort her children hugging them tight and checking them out for injuries. She grabbed her cellphone and dialed her sister, Shell.

An Uneasy Truth 2

"Hello," Shell answered on the second ring.

"Sista, are you home? I'm coming through," Isis said as she pulled out of the gas station into traffic headed to Shell's house.

"Yeah, I'm home. What's wrong?" Shell asked sensing the uneasiness in her sister's voice.

"See you in a few," Isis said before hanging up.

Chapter 2

*I*sis pulled up into Shell's driveway quickly and they got out. Shell was standing on her porch waiting and Lem and Sky ran to their aunt and hugged her tight.

"Y'all go ahead inside with y'all cousin. Me and your mama gotta talk," Shell said as she wiped the lone tears that streamed down her nephew's face. They did as they were asked then Isis and Shell sat down to talk.

"Sis, what the fuck is going on? My nephew is crying, and he doesn't even cry. What the fuck happened?" Shell shot questions off fast.

"Mann sis, somebody stabbed Troy and tried to beat him to death, and then Vee shows up at the hospital as I'm leaving and starts a fucking shoot out right there with the kids in the car. Shit is crazy I can't even begin to think who would do that shit to Troy," Isis said as she shook her head from side to side in disbelief.

"What the fuck? Are you serious? I'm calling Mel," Shell said as she ran into the house to get her cellphone.

"Hey Bro. Get over here ASAP I need to talk to you," Shell said, not even giving him a chance to get a hello out.

"Aight, I'm on my way." Mel said.

"Well Sista, I got something to share with you before Mel get here," Shell said as she looked her sister in the eyes.

An Uneasy Truth 2

"What's up?" Isis said as she looked at her sister suspiciously.

"I'm the one who had Markel's shops burned down," Shell said as she looked down the block for no particular reason.

"What!?" Isis asked in disbelief.

"Yup fuck that nigga, Karma is a bitch," Shell said nonchalantly.

"Damn sis. All this shit is a lot to fuckin' process. Does Mel know?" Isis said with her face buried in her hands.

"Nah, he don't know for sure, but he may have an idea that something is up though," Shell replied.

"Mommy! Daddy's on the news!" Lem yelled form inside the house. Shell and Isis both rushed inside to see the reporter flashing a picture of her kids' father on the screen stating he was wanted for the shootout at the hospital and was armed and dangerous. "How the fuck did he get out in the first place?" Shell thought aloud. The doorbell rang, and Shell went to answer it.

"Uncle Ill!" Lem yelled as he ran to hug his uncle.

"What's good my G?" Mel said as he embraced his oldest nephew.

"I need to talk to you," Lem whispered in Mel's ear as they hugged.

"Ok no problem lil man. Walk with me to my car, I got something for y'all" Mel said as he noticed the intense look in his nephew's eyes.

Isis' cellphone began to ring she saw it was her mother and answered the call.

"Hey mommy."

"Isis, Vaughn wants you to meet with him over here." Nadine said in a nervous tone.

"What? Mommy what are you talking about where did you get that information?" Isis asked trying to remain calm.

"He's sitting right here," Nadine said before the phone was snatched from her hand.

"Bitch, bring your ass over here and bring my fucking kids with you. If you don't come or you call the police I'ma kill this bitch you call a mama," Vee said before hanging up.

"Uncle Ill, that nigga gotta die. He hurt my mama," Lem said with an intense look of anger on his face as tears streamed down his face.

Mel had never saw his nephew cry so to see his tears and hear the clarity in his words he knew these were his nephew's true feelings. Mel grabbed Lem up in a tight hug and assured him he would make it right.

"WHAT!" Shell yelled, startling both Lem and Mel.

"What's going on?" Mel yelled as he rushed back to the porch where Isis and Shell sat.

An Uneasy Truth 2

"That bitch ass nigga got Mommy, talkin' bout he gonna fuckin' kill her if Isis don't come solo with the kids," Shell said with panic in her voice as she headed into the house to call Tate.

Mel picked up his phone, dialed a number, and waited until the person on the other end answered.

"What's good youngster?" a male voice answered.

"Meet me at my house. It's war time," Mel said before hanging up. He walked into the house kissed his sisters and niece then dapped up his nephews.

"Uncle Ill, take me with you please," Lem pleaded.

"Nephew, I can't take you with me, but I love you and I'ma make this right for you," Mel said as he headed to the bathroom before he left.

Ten minutes later, Tate pulled into the driveway with tires screeching and jumped out his truck, leaving it running with the keys still in the ignition. Shell came flying out of her house with a pistol in hand.

"Fuck dat ain't shit to discuss let's go!" Shell yelled as she hopped in the driver seat with Isis on her heels climbing into the passenger seat.

"Fuck!" Tate yelled in frustration.

"Dad, what's going on? Are we going too?" Jamier asked with a confused look on his face.

Tate walked to the front door and got eye level with his son, "We'll be back shortly lock the door and put the alarm on," Tate began.

"I got it, Dad. This is an emergency," Jamier said calmly, cutting Tate off. He then closed the door quick in Tate's face and locked it.

Tate was taken back by his son's actions but knew he had been schooled when he heard the door lock and feet take off away from it.

"Let's go Tate, we ain't got time to waste," Shell yelled as she began backing out of the driveway.

"Damn, how you gonna leave me in my truck?" Tate asked as he jumped in the back just before Shell took off down the block.

"Nigga, I'll leave Jesus if it's about my mama. No offense Lord, keep us covered," Shell said as she bent the corner of 17th and Benning.

Isis sat quiet the whole ride she had so many different things running lapse in her head like she had no clue what was about to go down with Vee or where her brother broke off to once news hit that Vee had her mother hostage threatening her life.

"I'ma go up alone y'all," Isis said as Shell parked.

"Fuck that sis. I can't even let you do that," Tate said as he loaded the two glock 40's he had stashed in the backseat.

"Yea sis, I don't think that's a good idea. Not only are you solo, but the kids aren't with you. His psycho ass could just off you and mommy on that fact alone," Shell added.

Isis reached over and hugged her sister tight. "I love y'all, but I gotta end this alone. If mommy not out here in 10 minutes, then come up," Isis said as she got out of the truck and proceeded to the building.

Isis saw what she thought was Mel's car parked a few cars down as she walked into the building, but she brushed it off and started up the stairs. It seemed as though everything moved in slow motion every step closer to her mom's apartment she got. She could hear her heartbeat in her ears as it slowed down and skipped beats. A large lump formed in her throat as she thought of how fucked up this scenario could end.

When Loco got the call from Mel, his young hitter, about wartime, he gladly obliged considering he knew the situation with Isis and Vee. As soon as he heard footsteps in the hallway of the building, he peeped out of the peep hole of the apartment next door from Nadine and saw Isis. Loco swiftly stepped out of the door just as she opened the door and followed her in.

"Lo what," Isis spoke low as she noticed him pop through the door, startling her as she turned to close it.

Loco quickly silenced her with a finger to the lips. "Stay calm and walk in as if I'm not even with you," he whispered. Isis nodded signaling she understood yet she was still confused as to why or how he even knew to be there. At this moment, it didn't matter because she felt a sense of calm rush over her as she continued into the apartment.

"Ma," she called out until she saw her mom sitting with her back toward the door on the couch.

"I'm ok, baby," Nadine said as she turned to face her daughter who rushed to her side.

"Bitch, where the fuck my kids at?" Vee said to Isis as he stood in the doorway of the kitchen with a pistol on his hip and a large kitchen knife in his left hand.

Loco stood in the blind side of the apartment entrance, waiting for the moment to pounce on Vee. Nadine sat still and calm though her heart told her this man may kill her and her daughter at any moment. She felt he phone vibrate once from the cushion of the couch where she stashed it when Vee walked into her kitchen.

"I asked you a question bitch, where is my fucking kids?" Vee asked, looking at Isis in disgust.

"Look Vee, this is between me and you. There is no need for my children to be here," Isis said with confidence as she hugged her mom. Nadine quickly glanced at the text that came through her cellphone.

It's a nice night to see the stars. Open your curtains, Mom. Nadine was a bit confused, but she knew now wasn't the time to ask questions or hesitate, so she did as her son suggested and walked over opening the curtains. This gave Mel a clear shot from where he was perched across the street.

Vee was so wired up he hadn't noticed Nadine opening the curtains, His patience for Isis had grown thin. He immediately snatched Isis up by her throat. "The fuck you thought I was playing with your dumbass," Vee said looking Isis in her now watery eyes.

An Uneasy Truth 2

"No, Vaughn. Stop!!" Nadine yelled as she rushed over and tried to help peel Vee's grip on her daughter's neck. Vee dropped the knife and pulled the .38 he had tucked on his waist and pointed it at Nadine's head, the barrel meeting the center of her forehead with force.

"Slow your role, youngster," Loco stepped out of the blindside of the doorway with his pistol drawn on Vee.

"Oh my God, Lo," Nadine said as she rushed to his side instantly feeling safe.

Isis was running low on air when the front door came flying open and she was dropped to the ground. She thought she had died when she heard Lem say "Hi Daddy."

Vee lowered his pistol, seeing his son with a pistol pointed in his direction with a red beam trained on the center of his black t-shirt. Lem, who was only 11, stood as tall as his little frame would allow as he kept his pistol on Vee and stepped inside closing the door behind him.

"Bitch, you got my flesh and blood turning against me," Vee said as he lifted his hand to punch Isis as she stood from the floor.

"BOWW!" a bullet went soaring from Lem's pistol, hitting Vee in the arm.

"Nigga, you will never hurt us again. I fucking hate you," Lem said disregarding any and every adult in the room. Loco stood with Nadine off to the side as they watched everything unfold, pistol still drawn. He couldn't believe the heart this little boy had but it didn't surprise him. It was in his blood.

"Son, I love you. Give Daddy the gun," Vee reached for Lem's pistol with his unwounded arm.

Lem curled up his top lip. He had no respect for a nigga that would raise his hand to a woman, let alone his Momma. He once had respect for Vee, he probably even worshipped the ground he walked on but in the moment, Lem was going to protect what was his. He wasn't about to stand there and let the no-good son of a bitch hurt his Momma any more than he already had.

"BOWW, BOWW, BOWW." Lem hit him twice; once in the shoulder once in the side. At the exact same time Lem's third shot rang off a head shot came flying through the open window striking Vee in the back of the head causing him to fall over in an awkward position instantly. Everything happened so fast no one realized he had been hit with four shots except Loco who watched the beam briefly come through the window. Nadine and Isis were so focused on Lem shooting Vee they paid no attention.

Isis dropped to her knees and hugged her son shielding his view of his father's lifeless corpse and all the blood that was now spreading all over the area rug in Nadine's living room, She tried to remove the pistol from Lem's hand, but he wouldn't let it go. He sat on the chair facing the window and just gazed at all the people walking around and cars going by with the pistol on his lap.

Loco pulled out his cell and dialed out. The phone rang once before Smurf picked up.

"Ayy bro. Send the cleaners to the courts ASAP," Loco requested.

An Uneasy Truth 2

"It's done," Smurf replied.

Nadine looked at her grandson and his unbothered expression, as if he had just killed a bug and not his father, a man who was half responsible for his existence. As he sat he listened to Isis ask him what seemed to be a million questions while pacing back and forth in front of him. It scared her to see him in a dark place like this.

He's only 11 years old this isn't for him, she thought to herself as she walked to the front door of the apartment to let Tate and Shell inside after hearing them fussing on their way up the stairs.

"Ma, you good?" Shell asked as she ran to embrace Nadine.

"Yes, I'm ok but that baby. Oh Lord Shell, Lem should have never been here," Nadine said with tears in her eyes.

"What you mean Ma?" Tate scrunched his face up. "We left all the kids at Shell's house,"

As they entered the living room, confusion cascaded over them while Lem sat on the couch; cradling the pistol. Vee was sprawled, lifelessly, on the floor.

Nadine was getting ready to explain what had transpired when eight cleaners rushed into the apartment. Their job was to get rid of all of the evidence. As a man and woman started to roll Vee's body over, the woman gasped and put her hand over her mouth.

"Val, you good?" Tron whispered.

"Damn, yea I need some air. I'ma get somebody else to help move this mu'fucka he too heavy," Valerie turned to rush out of the apartment.

Valerie's heart was pounding, and the vomit threatened to spew everywhere tickling her throat and causing her mouth to get watery, when she bumped into Isis. Any other time she would have spit venom at her or anyone else for that matter due to just bumping into and not saying excuse me first to her but, today, hurt, pain and confusion was overwhelming her.

"Excuse me," she said as she continued out the door making note of Isis' and the little boy who was still holding the pistol's faces. She had no clue who they were or why Vee was here dead.

Once she was outside, she stepped behind a large dumpster out of sight and broke down crying. Valerie was Vee's on again, off again chick and they had a 12-year-old son named VJ. As she sat squatted next to the dumpster with her vision blurry from her tears, all she *could think about was how she would deliver the news of Vee's death to their son.*

Had I known things would have gotten this far, I never would have given him any information on that bitch, Valerie thought as she struggled to push the vision of Vee's dead body out of her mind. Working at the trap house for Smurf and Loco had come in handy when Vee came home needing information on a woman never saying who she was to him or why he wanted contact with her had she known it would have ended up like this she would have never participated.

An Uneasy Truth 2

The last thing on Isis's mind was Valerie. She didn't give a fuck about anyone but Lem. She had watched her son grow up before her eyes. She was pissed at herself for putting him in a position where he thought he had to protect her or anyone else. She was mad as hell that he was now a criminal though not or ever will he be convicted if left up to her but has taken a life nonetheless. She never envisioned this for her child—not today, not ever. "How the hell did you get here? Where the fuck you learn to shoot a gun? How the fuck did your little ass get a gun any fucking way? Hello, Kalem Wise Monroe, I know you hear me speaking to you," Isis shot off questions getting more upset with each unanswered question.

"Where did that head shot come from?" Nadine asked herself in a low tone.

Buzz... Buzz... Shell's cell phone went off indicating a text Shell saw it was from Jamier and opened it and read it.

Uncle Mel said come to the house. Everybody!

"Let's go. Mel wants us to meet him at my house," Shell said as she snatched up Lem and removed the pistol from his hand, sticking it in her hoodie pocket as they all filed out of Nadine's apartment.

Lem made eye contact with Shell, giving her a nasty look she returns the stare with a look that said "I wish your little ass would." He knew better than to test her and made his way to the truck.

"Mommy, you are staying with us tonight," Isis said as she climbed into the backseat of the truck with Lem.

"That's fine, but I'm gonna ride with Loco to Shell's house," Nadine said as she sat in the passenger seat of Loco's tinted, black Cadillac.

"Aight Lo, just follow me over," Tate said as he pulled out of the parking lot. Shell reached to turn on the radio and began flipping through the stations it seemed like every station was on a commercial break.

"Let me deal with my tunes ma'am," Tate said laughing as he pressed play on the system and Scarface played the rest of the ride back to Shell's house.

Meanwhile in Loco's car, Nadine and Loco were having an intense conversation.

"I see my daughter isn't aware of the bloodline she's connected to," Loco said in a salty tone.

"Loco, we've have been having this conversation since the day she was born. I wasn't comfortable telling her when she was younger, and I damn sure ain't interested in telling her as a grown ass woman. I'd rather just let it be," Nadine said with her head hung in shame. She felt bad about the entire situation, but she had no regrets. It was one of those uneasy truths she wasn't ready to face.

"Nadine, its time. Look at what's going on around you. Granted when you found out you was carrying her I was in Cali and later got locked up in Texas but I'm back. We're back," he said, giving her an assuring hand squeeze as he drove.

"I guess you are right," Nadine said as she looked over into his eyes. One thing she knew for sure he was true about his word. Even locked up he made sure she and her kids got what they needed even the two that weren't his.

An Uneasy Truth 2

Nadine knew it was time her children knew the truth; well some of it at least.

Chapter 3
Way Back in the Day

"You'll be ok, sista. He's the fool," Pam said as she held and rocked her best friend Nadine as she cried on her shoulder.

"How could he do this to me?" Nadine cried. She couldn't believe Markel had cheated on her.

"That's his loss. Look here, we hangin' out tonight," Pam said as she stood up and pulled Nadine to her feet.

"I don't know Pam. I'm just not feeling social," Nadine said as she wiped the tears from her face.

"I'll be here to get you around nine Nadine. Be ready," Pam yelled over her shoulder as she walked away and climbed into her car and rolled down her windows. McFadden & Whiteheads' "Ain't No Stopping Us Now" blared through her little car speakers.

"You better be ready at nine. Don't make me have to pull you out of that house tonight," Pam shouted over the music.

"Ok Pam," Nadine laughed as she walked into the house knowing Pam meant exactly what she said. She would pull her out of the house.

Nadine walked past her mom as fast as she could to get to the steps that lead to her bedroom she couldn't let her see her crying about Markel not knowing she heard the entire conversation.

"You ok child? I heard you and Pam talking," Nadine's mom asked once she had started up the stairs.

"Yes mama, I'm fine," Nadine replied as she continued up the stairs to her bedroom.

"You should be living your life baby girl. Don't wait on that fool 'cause he gonna keep you in tears. You deserve better," Nadine's mom yelled up the stairs.

Nadine sat on her bed as her mothers words sank in and wrote a long letter to Markel then prepared her outfit for the night.

"Mama and Pam are right. He's the fool. I'ma enjoy my life. Fuck waiting around. I'm 19 and fine as hell," Nadine thought to herself as she admired her shape in the mirror, trying on her outfit.

Ringggg... Ringg... the house phone rang.

"Hello," Nadine's mom answered.

"How are you doing Mom? May I please speak to Nadine?" Markel asked politely.

Paula paused and pulled the receiver away from her face and balled her face up as if he could see her.

"Hell no! Markel, you got some fucking nerve calling my house after you had my child crying and shit. Your best bet is to stay the fuck away from my child and disappear," Paula yelled into the receiver before hanging up.

Nadine stood at the top of the stairs listening to her mom scream on Markel, feeling relieved that she had taken care of that situation but made a mental note to drop her letter off on her way out.

"Come help me with dinner," Paula said with a grin, noticing Nadine was standing at the top of the stairs.

Nadine smiled and joined her mom in the kitchen. They prepared dinner, said grace, and ate before Nadine headed back upstairs to get ready to head out with Pam.

Once she was dressed, she sat down at her vanity and braided her long wavy hair into a French braid, put a pair of diamond studs in her ear, and added some lip gloss.

"Ready," She said as she smiled at herself in the mirror.

"Nadine! Pam just pulled up," Paula shouted hearing Pam's music playing loud from her car outside.

"Ok Mama, thanks," Nadine said as she grabbed her clutch and headed out, kissing her mother on the cheek on her way out the door.

"Ok nowww!" Pam said with a smile.

"Hush girl. Where are we going?" Nadine blushed.

"Just a card party," Pam replied as she pulled off into traffic in route to her cousin's place.

"Swing by Markel's place I wanna drop this in his mailbox." Nadine said holding up the enveloped letter.

After dropping it off 10 minutes later They pulled up to a house in a live community uptown. From the looks of things, the card party was already live once they got inside. Pam introduced Nadine to a few of her family members and their friends that she didn't know. Nadine had started to enjoy herself laughing at constant jokes, listening to music, and playing cards.

"Here, sip on this," Pam said as she handed Nadine a cup with Long Island Iced Tea in it.

Nadine took a sip and her face frowned up immediately. "Ewww, what's this?" she asked trying to pass the cup back.

"Haa Haaa. Girl it's just a lil' Long Island. You don't like it?" Pam laughed as she took a toke of the joint that her big cousin Loco had passed her.

"Oh shit. Nadine, this is my big cousin Loco. He's from Cali. Loco this is my best friend," Pam said passing the joint back to Loco.

"How you doing, Miss Lady?" Loco said as he reached out to shake her hand.

"I'm good," Nadine blushed shaking his hand.

"You ain't wanna hit this?" Loco asked, attempting to pass Nadine the joint.

"No thanks, I'm good with this cup," Nadine replied as she felt the long island ice tea Pam gave her creeping up in her system. *Damn, it's getting warm in here,* she thought to herself.

An Uneasy Truth 2

"Ayy Loc! Domino game in effect bro, you in?" Smurf yelled from the kitchen.

"Hell yea," Loco said as he got up to join the game.

"Dominos?" Nadine asked in a puzzled tone.

"Don't tell me you don't know about dominos?" Loco joked.

Nadine began to feel a little embarrassed because she had never even heard of the game before. Loco gazed down at her and reach out his hand.

"C'mon you can watch me kick some ass on this table."

Pam grinned as she watched her girl hesitating. She slid over and whispered in her ear. "Get your ass on up. Time for some new shit," She said as she gave her a slight nudge off the couch.

Loco grabbed Nadine's hand to stop her from stumbling and lead her to the table, pulled out her chair, and introduced her to everyone. Pam sat on the couch sipping her drink, satisfied that she had made a good connection. Loco had approached her while Nadine was in the bathroom interested in who she was and what she was about. Pam informed him that Nadine was her best friend and she was out to get over somethings and he understood.

Nadine watched quietly and listened as Loco explain the game play by play. Now on cup number three, Nadine started to feel her buzz in full effect, her insides warm and tingly. She sat her cup down and looked at Loco as he rolled up another joint.

"Can you walk me outside? I think I need some air," Nadine asked with a slight slur in her words.

"Sure sweetheart," Loco said as he sat the half rolled joint down and escorted her through everyone dancing in the living room. Loco had already done his own personal evaluation of Nadine, so he noticed she was buzzed from cup number two which told him she didn't drink. She declined to hit the joint despite the fact everyone around her indulged and he liked that. Loco found it a turn off for a female to be wild and out there or a get with.

"You ok?" Loco asked as he pulled her up a chair to sit down while he took a seat on the porch steps in front of her.

"Yea, I think so. Hell nahhh, I'm drunk," Nadine giggled.

"Damn, you wanna go home? I can get cuz to take you right now," Loco said as he stood up to go get Pam to take her home.

"Nahh, I'm ok. I just wanna sit here and enjoy this night air," Nadine said as she pulled him to sit in the chair next to her.

"Ok, groovy," Loco said as he got up off the stairs and sat down in the chair beside her.

"Ayy Smurf!" Loco yelled through the open window he sat in front of.

"What's good?" Smurf said popping his head in the window.

"Bring me a glass of water please," Loco requested

An Uneasy Truth 2

"Gotchu," Smurf left and returned with a cool glass of water and handed it to Nadine. Nadine smiled and thanked him before he went back to the party.

"Thank you," Nadine said after taking a few sips of the water.

"No problem. I see this isn't really your setting," Loco smiled.

"Damn, so you do smile?" Nadine joked seeing he had one himself she hadn't seen him smile since she arrived.

"Sometimes," Loco replied honestly.

"Yeah because I've been kind of checking you out and noticed with all the fun going on around you, you didn't smile once. It's good to see you have one though," Nadine said with a smile.

Loco was 6 foot 3 the 180lbs with smooth caramel skin and honey eyes and a baby face.

"How old are you?" Loco asked.

"I'm 19. And yourself?" Nadine said.

"I'm 25. Is that too old for you?" Loco asked silently praying her answer was no.

"Maybe," Nadine laughed, she was low key impressed he definitely didn't look 25.

Loco was completely thrown off by her answer but played it cool. "I guess we'll have to find out then. Huh?" Loco said before walking inside to get Pam.

"Ayy cuz, Nadine said she ready to go." Loco said jokingly to Pam who was getting down on the floor with a light skin cat she was digging.

"Really?" Pam yelled from across the room not missing a beat.

"Now Pam wants to know are you ready to go? Whatever you say I'ma take as that answer. Maybe's don't count," Loco turned to Nadine and said with a grin.

Nadine was stuck. She wasn't ready to go home. *Guess that hard to get shit just backfired on me*, she thought to herself.

"No Loco, I'm not ready to go home yet," Nadine said with a laugh.

"Oh, false alarm cuz, she good," Loco laughed as he sat back down beside Nadine.

They sat on the porch laughing and talking alone until Pam came out saying she was ready to go.

They exchanged numbers and began to hang out often after that night. Even Nadine's mom liked having him around. She noticed the age difference but was completely fine with Loco and Nadine hanging out if he treated her daughter with the utmost respect and thus far he had. It was three months into them getting to know each other and Loco was feeling Nadine deeply and vice versa, they had gotten close, so he would sometimes just go hang out with her on her porch when she wasn't working, and he wasn't out of town. It was a peaceful Friday evening and like any day they were relaxing on Nadine's porch cracking jokes and talking with her mom before Paula went inside to use the restroom.

An Uneasy Truth 2

"Hey, take a ride with me," Loco said to Nadine as he took a seat on her front porch beside her. Nadine glanced at the screen door she could feel her mama's eyes on her.

"Go ahead," Paula chuckled.

"Ok, I guess," Nadine giggled as Loco grabbed her hand and led her down the steps.

"See you later, Mama," Nadine said after stepping back opening the door and hugging Paula.

"Ok love you. Y'all be safe now," Paula said as she closed the screen door smiling. She was glad to see her daughter happy. "because Lord knows that damn Markel ain't nothing but trouble and bullshit," she said to herself as she began to clean up the dinner dishes and put up the leftovers.

Loco and Nadine hit I-95 slow grooves played as they rode. Nadine began to dose off ten minutes into the ride. Loco chuckled he figured her day must have been long so he let her sleep the remainder of the ride, occasionally glancing over at her beautiful, brown face.

Once he reached their destination, he pulled into the driveway of a little house tucked off behind what seemed like thousands of trees, parked, and gently kissed Nadine's sleeping lips.

"Hey, Sleeping Beauty, we're here," he smiled as her eyes fluttered then slowly opened and met his.

"We're here?" she sleepily smiled.

"Yes, now come on. I wanna show you something," Loco said as he unfastened her seatbelt and walked around to open her door.

Nadine pulled herself together and climbed out of the car. *I don't know where we are but it's beautiful*, she thought to herself as she walked up the illuminated cobblestone pathway to the open front door. She asked no questions; she just walked in and took a seat on the plush floral pattern sofa that sat in the corner of the living room.

"You ok? Would you like something to drink?" Loco asked as he turned the radio on.

"Yes please," Nadine replied.

As Loco headed to the kitchen, Nadine took in all her surroundings. There were large beautiful paintings hanging on each wall inside the spacious living room. It was beautifully decorated with a black and gold theme. Loco walked up holding two glasses in his hands.

"Here you go."

"Thanks," Nadine said as she took a sip. "I love Cherry Coke," she said with a smile.

"Yeah, I know," Loco smiled back

Nadine sat her glass down and turned to Loco with a serious look on her face. Loco thought something was wrong but before he could ask, she had covered his mouth with her own, kissing him passionately. Loco was enjoying the moment but was in no rush with Nadine, so he stopped her.

"Listen to me," Loco said seriously as he looked her in her eyes.

"Yes Lo," Nadine asked in an innocent tone.

"You sure you wanna move further?" Loco asked, because he didn't want her to think this is what he brought her with him for. No sooner than the question left his lips, Nadine was on his lap. She felt nothing spoke better than actions as she began to place wet kisses behind his ear while she rubbed her fingers through his wavy hair.

Loco got up off the sofa and carried Nadine to his bedroom. Her answer couldn't get any clearer. He laid Nadine on his California King-sized bed and slowly undressed her, placing kisses all over her body. Nadine had never felt this way before. Thunderbolts were shooting through her love box. Loco slowly spread her legs and placed soft sloppy kisses on her clit. By the third kiss, she thought she would lose her mind it felt so good she had never experienced anything like this with Markel.

Loco slowly stuck two fingers into her love box. It was warm, wet, and tight so he was having a tough time containing himself and was ready to devour her box in ways she never imagined.

Nadine stopped him as her legs began to tremble. "I wanna feel you," she said as she pushed him on to his back and climbed on top of him. He was bigger than what she was used to, but she slid right on. He was snug like the perfect fit. They both moaned in ecstasy as Loco rolled over on top of her giving her slow passionate thrust looking deep into her eyes, they connected.

Nadine wrapped her arms and legs around Loco tightly as he got deeper inside her. She was loving the feeling he was giving her.

"Ooooooo don't stop. I'm about to cum.." Nadine moaned. She could feel her walls tightening around Loco's throbbing manhood. She lifted her hips to meet each thrust until she felt herself explode, squirting her juices up Loco's ripped abs and all over the sheets under her. That sent Loco over the edge causing him to explode inside of her.

"Damn. You just robbed me of a lifeline," Loco said in exhaustion as he rolled off Nadine and wrapped his arms around her keeping his manhood inside her.

"Damn, what?" Nadine giggled as she cuddled into Locos arms.

"You just robbed me with no gun," Loco replied with a laugh.

"What you mean?" Nadine asked seriously as she flipped over and looked into his eyes.

Loco burst into laughter seeing the seriousness in Nadine's face. "It doesn't matter. You so cute when you're confused."

Nadine was confused she had no clue what he meant by "stealing his lifeline". She had never heard that before. Loco saw that she was still pondering the statement.

"You'll get it in nine months," Loco said as he held her tight. He could feel his feelings growing for Nadine. He just didn't wanna rush it since she was fresh out of a situation with ol' boy. But if his prediction of her catching

An Uneasy Truth 2

his drift in 9 months came to fruition everything had sped up.

"I'm gonna act like u ain't say that," Nadine said as she punched Loco in the arm and got up to gather her clothes.

"You can but I know my strength lil woman," Loco said as he grabbed her up from behind and kissed all over her neck and shoulders.

"Where is the bathroom, Lo? You Mister Funnyman tonight I see. We gotta get going before mama get worried," Nadine asked with a slight laugh.

"Down the hall, second door on the right," Loco said as he crept up behind her just as she opened the door, he picked her up tossed her over his shoulder and tossed her back onto his king-sized bed.

"What if I'm not ready for you to leave yet?" He asked as they both burst into laughter and started wrestling on the bed. They laughed and wrestled for thirty minutes before Nadine got up and headed to the bathroom. When Nadine returned Loco was standing at the big bed room window lost in his thoughts as he gazed at the moonlit pond. He didn't hear Nadine creep up behind him. She gently wrapped her arms around him and began caressing his chest while she placed sensual kisses on his back.

"This is a beautiful view," Nadine said.

"Yeah thanks. It's one of the main reasons I bought this house," Loco said as he turned to look at Nadine. Nadine was impressed she didn't know any 25-year-old that owned a house or anything for that matter, but she asked no questions.

"You're beautiful, you know that?" Loco said with a smile as he kissed her forehead.

"Thanks, we should really get going," Nadine said as she blushed, she could feel her heart rate increase as they gazed into each other's eyes.

"Yeah, we should because I need Mama to trust me," Loco said as he put on his jeans. As he got dressed he couldn't take his eyes off Nadine.

"Ok, I'm ready," Nadine said in a perky tone as she walked into the living room and took another sip of her cherry coke. Loco didn't want her to go but he knew her mom would be worried, so he grabbed her hand and his keys then they headed out the door. He opened her door and as she started to get in, he grabbed her arm and snatched her back then kissed her passionately. Nadine was caught off guard but didn't protest and began kissing him back before she climbed into the car.

Their kiss was so intense Nadine debated in her head if she was ready to go home.

"What's wrong?" Loco said seeing that Nadine was in deep thought with a puzzled look on her face.

"Nothing at all. I love spending time with you. I just adore how you treat me," Nadine replied

"You my lady. I'm supposed to make you happy, right?" Loco asked with a smile as he picked up Nadine's hand and kissed the back of it softly.

Nadine smiled. "I guess so," she said as she turned up the volume on the radio and they rode back to her house. Once they finally arrived, Loco walked Nadine to her front door.

"I'ma see you later, ok?" Loco said as he lifted her in a warm embracing hug.

"That's cool," Nadine said with a smile as she leaned in and gave him a peck on the lips and hugged his neck. He placed her on her feet and started back down the stairs when suddenly the front door flew open.

"Goodnight Lo," Paula said sarcastically with a smirk on her face, one hand on her hip, and the other on the door knob. Nadine giggled as she grabbed her mom's hand from the door knob and pulled her inside. Loco smiled to himself while he walked back to his car. He drove around the corner to his apartment just as the sun began to rise and slept peacefully in his king-sized bed. Nadine sat and talked to her mom about where she had been and how much she was feeling Loco before she went up to her room. As she gathered her night gown and towel, she thought about what Loco had said once they had finish having sex, "You just robbed me of a lifeline", wondering exactly what that meant because she had never heard it before. As she stepped in the shower she allowed the hot water to cascade down her body as every moment with Loco replayed in her mind. She was digging him and clearly the feelings were mutual, and it was a good feeling. After washing and rinsing off she headed to her room, closed her door, and stretched out in her bed. Loco gave her butterflies. She drifted off to sleep with positive vibes about Loco.

Ding dong, Nadine was awakened by her doorbell being rung repeatedly. She jumped out of bed and stormed down the stairs to the front door and without looking out the peephole yanked the door open and screamed "Whaaaaaaaaaaaaaat!?!?"

"Damn, Nadine. I just wanted to check on you," Markel said, taken back by her greeting.

"Well maybe you should try calling first before popping up on people's door step," Nadine replied with her hand posted on her hip and attitude dripping from every word she spoke.

"Can I come in, so we can talk?" Markel asked with a pitiful look on his face.

"Nahh we can talk on the porch. Let me get dressed," Nadine said as she turned around to head back upstairs. Just as the door began to close Markel caught it and stepped inside. He closed and locked it then quietly crept up the stairs toward Nadine's bedroom where she was bent over stepping into her shorts Just as she began to pull them over her knees Markel wrapped his one arm around across her breast and the other around her waist holding her tightly.

"I've missed you baby, the way you feel inside, your touch, your smell." He said as he slowly rubbed his fingers across her exposed pussy while slowly tongue kissing her neck. Nadine fought for a few minutes but what he was doing to her was feeling good. She could feel her inside ache to be touch with each stroke of his finger across her throbbing clit'.

"Kel I ca.." She began to say but the erotic wave he had he body on had her questioning her better judgement.

"I need you," Markel said as he lifted Nadine off her feet and swiftly removed her shorts from around her calf and placed her on her bed as he kissed her seductively. Before she knew it, he was inside of her soaking wet love box, slow stroking and whispering I'm sorry in her ear.

Nadine was on a forbidden high, he felt so good inside her, Markel being her first and only until Loco knew where to touch and kiss her without effort.

"You driving me crazy you feel so good Nay, have my baby." Markel moaned in Nadine's ear.

Nadine was on her own euphoric high she had tuned his words out and was only listening to the tune of his body as he hit her spot and she began to squirt up his stomach and shirt and all over her sheets under her.

"Get the fuck out Markel," Nadine yelled as she began to come to her senses she grabbed her shorts and quickly put them on.

"What? Why you acting like that?" Markel questioned as Nadine began to push him out her room and down the hall.

"You think because you come over here and tell me all the shit you think I wanna hear, everything is alright? Nope it's not," Nadine yelled angrily as she pushed him toward the stairs.

"I love you. You think I just came over here to fuck? No! I want you in my life. I want to be with you," Markel pleaded as he stumbled down the stairs a bit.

"Fuck that. What I look like I got a Boston baked bean for a brain? I'm done," Nadine yelled as she pushed a barely clothed Markel out of the front door and on to the porch.

"And you might wanna put your pants on and go home before my mama pull up and fuck you up for being half naked on her porch," Nadine said as she slammed the door in Markel's face.

She slid down the door and onto the floor and broke into tears. "How could I be so fucking dumb," she thought to herself and she replayed the incident in her mind.

After a few minutes, she ran upstairs, showered, and scrubbed her skin until it was sore. She just wanted to erase any trace of his touch. After her shower, she dressed and call her best friend Pam to come over. Just as she hung up, she noticed her mom had prepared breakfast for her and left a note it read "*Out with cousin Karla. Be back soon baby love. -Mommy*"

I can't stand Karla. Family or not she ain't no good, she thought to herself as she stuck her plate in the oven to warm her food. As she waited for her food to warm up, there was a rhythmic knock at the door she knew it wasn't anyone but Pam but decided to check just in case.

"Heyy now," Pam greeted Nadine with a smile and warm hug as she opened the door. Nadine hugged her back and closed the door and locked it. Once Pam stepped inside she started telling Nadine what her night was like.

An Uneasy Truth 2

"Oooooo breakfast," Pam said with excitement, cutting her story when she watched Nadine pull her plate out of the oven.

"You want some? I'm not all that hungry," Nadine said as she sat the plate and a fork on the placemat in front on Pam. Pam dove face first into the plate and after eating a few minutes, she noticed Nadine wasn't talking. When she looked up at her, she saw the tears streaming down her cheek. After taking a few more bites of food she got up grabbed Nadine's hand and led her upstairs to her room. Nadine stretched across the bed and cried into her pillow as Pam closed and locked the door.

"What happened?" Pam asked as she sat next to Nadine.

"I fucked up," Nadine said before she began to tell her what happened from the previous night with Loco to that morning with Markel.

"So that mu'fucka raped you?" Pam asked with aggression in her tone.

"I can't say that cause I let him do it and for a split second I thought I felt something then I thought of Loco. I really care for Loco. I fucked up, and he gone find out and never wanna talk to me again," Nadine expresses as she pouted with her head hung and tears streaming down her face.

"No he not Nadine cause he ain't gonna never know. You can care for somebody, hell love them even, and not tell them every aspect of your life. Just don't let that shit happen no more," Pam said as she hugged her best friend and wiped away her tears.

"You right. My emotions all mixed up right now. Markel is done now Let's go watch some TV, " Nadine said as she hugged Pam then got up to walk out of the room. She loved her best friend she always knew what to say and how to say it.

They walked down stairs and watched TV in the living room, giggling and laughing for hours before Pam realized it was 3 o'clock.

"I gotta go run a few errands for aunt Sharon. I'ma swing back by around nine to get you," Pam said as she got up to leave.

"Ok cool. And thanks again," Nadine said as she walked Pam to the door. Just as she opened the door, her mom was coming in.

"Hey girls," she said as she rushed pass them both headed to the bathroom.

"Heyy Ma!" Pam shouted on her way out the door.

Nadine locked the front door then walked up stairs to her room to find an outfit for the night. She tried on three different outfits and still had not found the right one.

"Whatchu doing baby?" Paula asked as she watched Nadine rotate shirts and skirts on her bed.

"Hey Mama, I'm just trying to find something nice to wear. I'm going out with Pam tonight," Nadine said holding a black tank top up to her neck and a dark blue denim knee length skirt to her waist.

An Uneasy Truth 2

"Oh really? How you know I didn't have anything planned for us?" Paula asked with a smirk.

"Oh, Mama I'm sorry. I can call her right now," Nadine said feeling bad that she hadn't checked with her mom first. When Nadine's dad suddenly died three years ago, she and her mom clung to one another. They were one another's best friend and did lots of things together.

"Go on child. Have fun I'll be just fine. I'ma go on back over to Karla's house and play some cards," Paula said with a smile as she walked over and gave Nadine a hug. It warmed her heart to see that even though her child had a life she was willing to pause that just to spend time with her.

"Why your eyes look puffy? You been crying today?" Paula asked with a puzzled look as she stepped back and looked at her child.

Nadine didn't wanna tell the entire truth, so she covered with a half-truth. "Yea mama earlier when Pam and I were watching this really funny show, I may just need a nap," Nadine replied with a grin.

"Oh, ok well go ahead and get you one in before you go out. I know you sure are glad you got these two days off from work to get some rest and hang out with Pam and Loco, I'ma whip us up some food and wake you when it's ready."

"Okay Mama," Nadine said as she laid her clothes on the foot board of her bed and stretched out on her bed within minutes she had dozed off.

"Heyy the food is ready," Nadine heard someone whispering in her ear. She rolled over to see Loco smiling at her.

"Loco what you doing here? What time is it?" Nadine asked with a smile as she reached up and rubbed the side of his face.

"I'm here to pick you up beautiful. It's about nine o' clock." He replied with a smile as he sat beside her on the bed.

"Huh? Pam is supposed to pick me up," Nadine said in confusion.

"Yeah I know. She sent me instead now let's get downstairs and eat before we leave. Looks and smells like your mom threw down in there," Loco said as he grabbed her hand and assisted her to her feet.

"Cool, I'm hungry," Nadine said as she grabbed Locos hand and walked downstairs.

"I see you were able to wake her," Paula joked.

"I don't sleep that hard Mama," Nadine laughed.

"Yes, you do. I been up there three times trying to wake you up," Mama joked.

"Dang really? I must have been tired," said Nadine.

"Yes, I see. That's why I sent Loco I knew he would get the job done," Paula laughed.

"Well I'm woke now so feed me woman," Nadine joked as she washed her hands and took a seat at the table.

An Uneasy Truth 2

"What you still standing for honey? Have a seat so you can eat," Paula told Loco.

"Yes ma'am," Loco said with a smile as he sat across from Nadine. Paula served baked barbeque chicken, potato salad, fried cabbage and cornbread.

"Mmmmmmm mmmmm, Mama you sure did put your foot in this," Loco said in between bites.

"Aww thank you sweetie," Paula blushed. She liked Loco. It was something about him. His mature, charming, charismatic aura spoke volumes to her.

"No, thank you for sharing your meal with me," Loco stood up to remove his empty plate from the table.

"Oh, leave that Lo, I'll get it," Paula said as she stood and collected the empty dishes from the table.

"I'ma run upstairs and get dressed. I'll be right back,"

Nadine ran up the steps to her room, grabbed everything she needed then rushed into the bathroom, took a quick shower, brushed her teeth, applied lotion to her skin and then she got dressed. She went into her room to check herself over in the full-length mirror, dabbed some of her favorite perfume on before grabbing her clutch and heading down the stairs.

"That was fast," Paula walked out of the kitchen to have a seat on the sofa. Nadine giggled because she knew she would usually take a while to get ready to go anywhere.

"You look beautiful," Loco complimented, admiring her skirt; it hugged her curves.

"Aww Thanks Lo. I'm ready when you are," Nadine blushed.

"Ok, see you later Ma," Loco said to Paula as he and Nadine walked out of the front door.

"Y'all have a good time," She kissed Nadine on the cheek just before going back inside to get ready to leave.

"You look good baby girl." Loco said in Nadine's ear as he ushered her into the car.

"Thanks," Nadine blushed as she reached over to unlock his door.

Loco hopped in and they were off to the party. Markel stood at the corner of Nadine's block off in the shadows with anger in his heart as he watched them drive off.

The party was in full effect when they pulled up, Loco found parking two doors down from the house and they walked back to the party holding hands.

"You look really nice baby," Loco said to her as the strolled.

"Thanks, handsome, you too," Nadine blushed. Loco gave her a positive vibe and she was digging that.

"Hey now," Pam yelled from the hood of her car, happy to see her friend. Nadine walked over to her and gave her a hug.

"Hey yourself. This is sexy," Nadine said admiring Pam's skin-tight leather mini dress outfit.

An Uneasy Truth 2

"Yeah cuz, that's one badass dress," Loco complimented as he walked up and gave her a hug.

"Thank you love, y'all want a drink? We got plenty," Pam said as she led them inside.

"Sure do," Loco said as he locked fingers with Nadine and they walked through the crowd, both smiling and greeting familiar faces. There was a domino game going on to the left in the living room, a spades game going on in the kitchen, and a dice game going on in the basement the party was live.

Pam passed Nadine a wine cooler while Loco fixed himself a Hennessy and Coke then kissed Nadine before stepping off and joining the domino game.

"C'mon walk with me out back," Pam said grabbing Nadine's hand as they moved through the crowd and into the backyard. They both sat on the swing, Pam lit a joint she had rolled and began to rock the swing slowly back and forth as Nadine sipped her wine cooler and stared at the stars.

"I miss my Cali family," Pam said as she took a puff of her joint.

"I know you do. It used to be a time you were never in D.C and always out west. I wouldn't mind going out there with you to see what all the hype is about," Nadine giggled but soon noticed her friend wasn't laughing with her.

"What's wrong Pam?" Nadine asked in concern seeing that just talking about home brought her friend's mood down.

"I left somethings behind out there, Sis. I really need to get out there," was all Pam said as she gazed at the stars lost in her thoughts.

"Well, baby what's stopping us? We can go the week after next. I'll be off work since they are renovating at my job," Nadine said as she slid closer to her best friend as she playfully bumped her hip into Pam's, hip knocking her out of her daze.

"Really? You would go with me?" Pam said surprised that Nadine suggested they go the week after next week.

"What? You stoned. Put this shit out," Nadine laughed as she snatched the joint from Pam's lips and tossed it across the yard. "Look you are my best friend and it's rare that you daze into space talking about home like you just did, something is calling you through your soul so yeah we going to California," Nadine said as she hugged her Pam around the shoulder.

Pam was at a loss for words. What Nadine was saying was every bit of the truth. Something was calling her soul and that something happened to be Pam's one-year-old son she'd left there. She was glad to have a friend so wise.

"You gotta make sure you talk to your mom first. We gonna be gone a whole week and we don't need her putting no missing person report out." Pam laughed as she hugged Nadine.

"The week after next it is," Nadine said as she tossed back the remainder of her wine cooler and smiled

An Uneasy Truth 2

"Well since you done tossed my joint I gotta go get another one lets head in."

As they were walking inside Loco walked right into them. "Hey now, I been looking for you," he said to Nadine as he gently grabbed her hand and pulled her in to his embrace.

"There y'all two go again," Smurf teased as he walked into the kitchen to fix himself a shot of tequila.

"Aww shut your mouth Smurf," Pam laughed as she sealed her joint. Nadine grabbed another wine cooler and sipped it slow while the four laughed and held friendly conversation.

"I'm about to head to this spades table with my sexy partner," Loco said as he picked up his refilled glass of Hennessy and Coke with one hand and grabbed Nadine's tiny hand with his other.

"Cool, I'm headed out to the backyard to engage with the stars," Pam said with her perfectly rolled joint in her hand walking out the back door.

"Wait up Pam," Smurf yelled as he caught the back door just before it closed as he ran to catch up with Pam.

Nadine and Loco teamed up against his two cousins, Alicia and Hamid, who talked trash the entire game while getting spanked by Loco and Nadine. Nadine had already begun to feel the buzz of her sixth wine cooler.

"I need some air Lo," Nadine said as she laid her hand of cards on the table. Loco got up and escorted his lady out to get some air as she asked.

"Oh, now y'all mu'fuckas wanna run out when I get a decent hand," Alicia said jokingly as Loco and Nadine walked out the front door. The party continued, and the next players took their seat at the card table.

Nadine took a seat on the steps in front of the house feeling a little sick to her stomach, so she just folded her arms across her knees and rested her head on top of them. "If you need to lay down, there's a bed upstairs," Loco said as he sat next to her rubbing her back.

"Nahh, I think I just need some air besides I'm not even tryna be the party pooper as Pam would say," she laughed weakly.

"You damn right 'cuz I ain't no party pooper," Pam said loudly with laughter as she popped up from around the side of the house.

"That's just like yo' ass to be lurking around some corner," Nadine laughed. She loved her best friend Pam because she was the closest thing she had to a sister.

"What's going on out here? Ewww, you look like you need more than some air baby girl," Pam said as she felt Nadine's forehead.

"I know you need to cut that shit out," Nadine said, smacking Pam's hand down from her forehead.

"See, that's two votes to one, guess you know what that means," Loco said as he stood from the steps and reached for Nadine's hand.

"Fine," Nadine said as she reached up and grabbed Loco's hand with a fake attitude.

An Uneasy Truth 2

Pam smiled. She loved seeing her friend like this. Happy, not just because it was her blood, but because she genuinely cared about Nadine and that's what she needed after dealing with Markel.

"Alright cuz, I'll catch you tomorrow," Loco said as he hugged Pam.

"Sure thing, and take care of my girl," she replied with a sly grin knowing he would.

"I can take of myself just fine, thank you," Nadine said with sass as she snatched Pam into a hug they both laughed.

Loco and Nadine headed to Loco's car hand in hand. She felt at peace as they both climbed into his car and pulled off into the night with slow jams playing during the ride. They rode holding hands on and off as Loco maneuvered the wheel through the city. He had no specific destination in mind nor did Nadine say where she wanted to go. All he knew was he was comfortable and at peace with her just as she was with him.

"Lo where we going?" Nadine asked as she gazed out the window.

"Wherever you wanna go lil' mama," He replied sincerely.

Nadine said nothing and just reclined her seat and got comfortable. She remembered from their previous trip to his home that the ride was long. It's like Loco read her mind as he jumped on the beltway and headed to his house in the cut. Once they arrived, Loco looked over at Nadine and she was knocked out. He laughed to himself as he got out and walked to the front door of the house to unlock and open the door. Once he did, he walked back to the passenger door, opened it, and carefully unlatched Nadine's seatbelt. She didn't even flinch. He carefully lifted her seat and carried her inside. He laid her on the bed and removed her shoes, then he went and got a small trash can that was sitting near his bedroom door and brought it near the bed just in case. He then grabbed a ginger ale from the fridge and sat it on the end table nearby. He removed his shirt and shoes while he sat at the end of the bed and watched Nadine sleep a few minutes. He walked over to the large window and stood there a few minutes lost in his thoughts as he admired the peaceful atmosphere.

"Come lay with me," Nadine said sleepily as she wiggled out of her skirt and got comfortable in his bed. Loco walked over and climbed into the bed and held Nadine, this complete feeling she gave him was like nothing he had ever felt. He snuggled his face between her shoulder and neck, taking in her scent. Soon they both had fallen into a deep, comfortable slumber. The sun was creeping over the tall trees and peeping into Loco's window when it caressed Nadine's face.

"Oh, shit Lo!" Nadine said as she jumped out of the bed and quickly slid on her skirt.

"Huh? What's wrong?" Loco groggily asked, barely waking from his sleep.

"Lo, its morning. My mama is probably worried sick, I gotta get back," Nadine said in a shaky tone as she ran around the room in circles looking for her shoes.

Loco laid there with his eyes closed taking in what Nadine said. Within seconds he had fully processed what she'd said, he got up quickly and retrieved Nadine's shoes that she was still running around in circles looking for. He didn't want any issues with Ms. Paula. She trusted him with Nadine and he respected her very much.

"I got 'em Lo, let's go. Oh my God my mama must be goin' crazy right now," Nadine said as she quickly put on her shoes and headed for the door with Loco on her heels, he was hopping around to put his shirt and shoes on as he trailed behind Nadine.

They jumped into Loco's car and sped up the road, both of their minds running wild with thoughts of how Nadine's mother might be worried or worse called the police.

When Loco pulled up they both got out of the car in a hurry and raced up the steps but were stopped dead in their tracks by Paula. She sat calm and collected, sipping her morning coffee on the porch in her fuzzy robe and slippers.

"Mama I'm so sorr.." Nadine began to apologize but her words were cut off by Paula raising her hand in the air, dismissing Nadine's apology.

"Good morning, go on inside," Paula said as her eyes left Nadine and landed on Loco with an evil glare. Nadine did as she was told and went inside.

Paula stared at Loco. She had been gathering her thoughts all night long. She liked him but what she wouldn't tolerate is him taking that for granted. Loco never meant to keep Nadine out. He had all respect for Paula and would never purposely violate her trust.

"Now son I like you a lot, and I'm not even gonna ask an explanation because I trust my daughter with you and I trust the decisions you both make are responsible ones," Paula said in a gentle yet stern tone, making full eye contact with Loco as she sipped her coffee.

"Yes ma'am. I would never violate your trust. I respect you and Nadine," Loco exclaimed.

"Know this Lo, that's my only child and I will kill for her," Paula said looking him directly in the eye. The look gave him chills, but he understood.

"Ms. Paula, nothing else needs to be said. I get your drift," Loco said as he walked up and hugged Paula. She embraced him back and Loco went on his way. He had love for Ms. Paula and the upmost respect for her, however, he was falling for Nadine and hard.

Nadine watched from her bedroom window as Loco got into his car and pulled off. She felt bad for spending the night out without calling her mom but her mother's calm and collected demeanor let her know that Paula liked Loco because had it been Markel, the police, search dogs and her uncles would've been out hunting her down and ain't no telling what her uncles would've done to him. Nadine laughed to herself as she gathered the items she needed for her shower. She was lost in her own thoughts, so she hadn't heard Paula enter the room.

"This amuses you," Paula said breaking Nadine's thoughts.

Nadine lowered her head, "Not at all mama." She hesitated.

"I'm going to get straight to the point, we have had an understanding for some time now and I won't have any misunderstandings due to new friendship. Last night was unacceptable and it won't happen again, understood?" Paula said with her hands on her curvy hips as she stared Nadine directly in her eyes.

Nadine knew she had made a mistake that could've been prevented with a simple phone call. "Yes ma'am," she replied as she dropped her head. Paula walked over and lifted her child's head by her chin and pecked her on the cheek, embraced her in a warm hug and left the room just as quietly as she'd entered. Nadine grabbed her things and headed to the shower, got in, scrubbed up, rinsed her body clean, got out, and dried off. She then applied lotion to her entire body then threw on some sweat shorts and a t-shirt. She climbed into her bed and dozed off.

Paula sat in her room thinking. She replayed Nadine's childhood up until the current day and smiled she was blessed and proud to have such a self-sufficient, sweet, obedient daughter. She looked up to the heavens "Wish you were here with us," she said to herself as she shed a tear with a smile. Paula missed her late husband and watching Nadine and Loco gave her a warm feeling. They reminded her of herself and Floyd, Nadine's dad and Paula's late husband.

Ring, ring, ring, "Hellooo," Nadine playfully sang into the receiver

"Hey Hey Hey." Pam greeted with a laugh.

"Hey Pam, What's goin' on?" Nadine asked taking a seat on the sofa, happy to hear from her best friend. It had been a couple days since she saw or heard from her which was usual for her since she was always on the move.

"Well remember at the party we were talking about going to Cali?" Pam asked while trying to keep her excitement under control.

"Yeaaaaaah, What's up with it?" Nadine asked with a puzzled look on her face.

"Fix your face," Paula said to Nadine as she walked pass her headed into the kitchen.

"Heyy Mama Bear," Pam shouted through the receiver after hearing Paula in the background.

"Mama, Pam says hello. Girl get to it already," Nadine said.

"Okay, Okay… so what does your week look like? Because Lo paying for our tickets, round trip expenses paid for a week," Pam said with elevated hype.

"Oh my God! Really?" Nadine asked in disbelief, she hadn't spoken to Loco since the day he dropped her off after they accidentally had a sleepover.

"Dead serious. So, go ahead and put that leave in at your job. We're leaving Thursday," Pam said with a smile. She knew this caught Nadine off guard.

An Uneasy Truth 2

"Damn girl, today is Monday. Let me talk to Mama first. My birthday is next week, and I don't wanna say yes if she had plans for me," Nadine said in a disappointed tone. She was excited about Cali and this trip is exactly what she needed considering the store she worked at closed earlier than expected for the renovations a week ago.

"Duhh, I know when your birthday is. Duh." they both laughed, "Ok that's even more reason I'll give you time to talk to Mama Bear today. I'll be around sometime tomorrow," Pam said.

"Okay, see you tomorrow," Nadine said as she hung up the phone. She thought for a few minutes about how to talk to Paula about her going to California. Just as she was about to get up Paula walked into the living room.

"What is wrong with your face?" Paula asked as she took a seat in the adjacent recliner.

"Oh, nothing Mama. I was just thinking," Nadine said as she sat back on the sofa. She knew a confused stank face would get her mama's attention.

"Well get it off your mind because it's making your face do weird stuff," Paula joked as she surfed the channels on the television.

Nadine giggled at her mother's words they caught her off guard. "Soooo Pam called me and invited me to go to Cali with her for a week and we leave Thursday," Nadine said as she crossed her toes in her shoes in hopes that her mother would be willing to let her accompany Pam.

"Oh really? What you packing?" Paula asked in a nonchalant tone as she smiled at Nadine.

"Oh my God Mama. Thank you!!" Nadine leapt from the sofa directly into Paula's lap like a big baby. She was happy her mother trusted her enough to go across country solo. Paula saw no harm in letting Nadine go with her best friend. Her recent job had unexpectedly closed for renovations early, and she didn't want to see her cooped up in the house or getting intertwined with Markel again by chance. She hated him with a passion and honestly wished Nadine had never met him.

The next day, Nadine got up and cleaned the house early before her mother woke up. Once she was done, she cooked breakfast-bacon, scrambled eggs with cheese, grits and pancakes. Paula's nostrils were invaded by the delicious smell of food. She got up and joined Nadine downstairs. Just as she entered the kitchen, Nadine was fixing their plates.

"Good morning Mama," Nadine said with a smile.

"Good morning sunshine. Breakfast smells delicious," Paula said with a warm smile as she hugged her daughter.

"Well what can I say? I learned from the best," Nadine said with a giggle as she sat their plates on the table. They both sat down and enjoyed breakfast while talking about Nadine's upcoming trip with Pam to California.

Ding dong, Ding dong.

An Uneasy Truth 2

The doorbell rang as Nadine began to wash the breakfast dishes. She stopped and dried off her hands to go answer the door, however, Paula beat her to it. Once she saw that her mom had it, she went back to continue the dishes.

"Hello Ms. Paula, may I speak with Nadine please," Markel politely asked with a sad look on his face trying to gain her pity. He secretly hated that Paula answered the door and not Nadine.

"Little boy, I know you better remove yourself from my porch and not just fast but with the quickness." Paula said in a calm tone.

"Ma'am, I just want to talk to her," Markel stuttered.

"LEAVE MARKEL!!" Paula's voice boomed, causing Nadine to drop a plate. She had never heard her mother's voice roar like that, so she hurried to the door to see what was going on. When she got to the door she froze in disbelief. She couldn't believe Markel had the nerve to show his face on her mama's doorstep after the last time he came by. Nadine instantly flew into a rage forgetting her mama was even standing there.

"Get the fuck off my mama's porch!" Nadine screamed at Markel.

Paula was taken back because she didn't know the child could get so loud. *Like mama like daughter I guess*, Paula laughed to herself inside.

"Look, I just came to talk, please hear me out," Markel pleaded.

"Fuck you and that talk. Excuse me Mama," Nadine said as she pulled her mother back inside and closed the door in Markel's face.

"Mama next time look out the peephole please." Nadine said as she went back to the kitchen and cleaned up the broken glass.

Paula laughed, "Look out the peephole huh?"

"Yes, I learned that for myself from the last time he popped up over here," Nadine said, cutting off the whole story. She knew if she'd told her mama what really happened, Markel would come up missing for sure and she wouldn't be going to California with Pam.

Paula laughed to herself once Nadine went upstairs as she replayed the entire situation from the door. "Baby, if she don't hold our traits."

"Mama what you laughing at?" Nadine asked startling Paula.

"You. Me. Your daddy," Paula replied with a smile.

"I miss him, too, mama," Nadine said as she sat next to Paula and hugged her tight.

Paula smiled as she looked at her beautiful daughter and shed a single tear. Nadine saw the tear and wiped it away. "Mama its ok, I love you we got each other," Nadine said as she too dropped a single tear. This was true, but Paula could see her daughter growing and her eventually being alone and it saddened her a bit, but she wasn't going to stunt her daughter's growth.

An Uneasy Truth 2

"Yes, baby it is ok. And I love you too," Paula said kissing her softly on the cheek and wiping her tears away. She got up and went to her room and returned fully dressed with her purse and shoes.

"Mama, where are you going?" Nadine cut off her conversion on the phone and asked.

"Just to run a few errands. I'll be back later. I love you," Paula said as she dashed out the door.

"Well dang, love you too," Nadine said into the air as the door shut.

"Yeah Trish me and Pam going to Cali in a day or so," Nadine told her older cousin who was on the phone.

"That is so exciting, need a chaperone?" Trish asked jokingly. She knew her little cousin didn't need one but if she wanted one she wasn't gonna turn down the offer.

"Hell, why not." Nadine replied

"What? Are you for real?" Trish asked in shock.

"Yeah if you can pay your own way," Nadine said

"Oh, honey that's not a problem. When do we leave?" Trish said as she walked over to her bed and lifted the mattress, retrieved six thick stacks of bills and began counting out six thousand dollars.

"We leave Thursday. Just come over Wednesday night because I'm not sure what time we leaving Thursday," Nadine said

"Groovy. See you Wednesday night," Trish said before disconnecting the call to pack and prepare for the trip to California.

Somewhere in a hood in Cali…

"You think I wanted to be somebody damn mama? Take they asses with you back to big bad D.C. You come bring your ass up in here like you king of some shit. Jive ass turkey," Michelle yelled angrily as spit flew from her mouth. She was filled with rage about Loco coming back to California calling himself chastising her about their twin daughters, Melanie and Mahogany.

Loco stood at the front door and listened as Michelle ranted on and on. "Look I'm just here to make sure the girls get what they need outta this mutha'fucka for real. On some real shit, go have a seat some fuckin' where," Loco said through gritted teeth. He was fuming; not only because she was a half ass mother, but she had the nerve to be popping slick out the mouth.

"Mel & Ma-ma let's go!" Loco's voice boomed. He had even startled Michelle into silence.

"But Dad, I'm still looking for my doll. I know I left it here," Mahogany.

"I'll buy you a new one. Let's go I can't take this shit no more," Loco said heading for the door.

"Of course, you running just like you always do. I should have known better than to have kids with you." Michelle yelled in his face.

An Uneasy Truth 2

Melanie and Mahogany stared at their mother with disgust. She always talked horribly about their father and they were growing tired of her.

"Let's go daddy," Melanie said grabbing Loco's hand and leading him the rest of the way to the door. It angered him how she could stand there and throw stones when in fact she wasn't even raising Melanie and Mahogany. His grandmother was and had been when she dropped them off on her doorstep ten years ago, two weeks after they were born.

Michelle asked to get them from time to time but for raising the girls, she couldn't really take credit for. Loco bounced from state to state but recently his grandmother had fallen ill so he had been in California more often than his usual bi-weekly visits.

"Yeah Daddy let's go, she ain't worth it," Mahogany said walking over to where her sister and father stood.

"You little bitch, you ain't worth it," Michelle spat as she rushed Mahogany and slapped her to the floor. Loco just reacted, smacking Michelle so hard she flew into the bookshelf, causing all the shelves to collapse.

"Oh my God." Melanie whispered.

"Fuck that Dad lets go," Mahogany said, snatching Melanie by the collar and heading out the door, leaving Michelle unconscious on the floor. Loco followed behind the twins and shut the door behind him while wiping off the handle with his sleeve in the same motion. As soon as they got to the car, they hurriedly got in and Loco pulled away from the curb.

"I'm sorry girls," Loco said, shifting his eyes between both girls in the rear-view mirror and the road.

"For what Daddy? You did what you had to do," Mahogany said, making eye contact with Loco through the mirror.

"No matter how far your mother goes or what she does or any female for that matter, I as a man should never get outta character and put my hands on them because I would never ever want a nigga to do y'all that way," Loco said in a calm tone as he pulled to the stop light and turned around to look his daughters in the eye.

"Daddy she just slapped my sister for telling the truth. She's not worth losing us. 'Cause if you kill her you would be gone for the rest of our lives," Melanie emotionally stated as she hugged her twin.

"Bitch would've loved that though," Mahogany mumbled in a low tone to her sister. "You were protecting us Daddy so you ain't gotta be sorry," She said to Loco. Loco nodded and continued to drive to his grandmother's home.

Once they arrived, the girls jumped out the car and ran up to the porch where their great-grandmother sat in a chair enjoying the evening air.

"Hey baby dolls!" she exclaimed as she hugged them both at the same time. G-ma Betty loved her some Mahogany and Melanie, they meant the world to her.

An Uneasy Truth 2

Loco sat in the car for a few minutes contemplating the scenario from Michelle's apartment and if things could've gone differently. *Tap Tap Tap.* Melanie broke Loco's thoughts tapping on the passenger window. He glanced over rolling the window down and silently thanked God for his twins.

"Dad, G-ma said you gonna just sit and stare into space or come love on her?" Melanie asked innocently with a grin.

Loco climbed out of the car and walked around to Melanie and threw his arm around her shoulder, pulling her close as they walked up to the porch together.

"Well hello there," G-ma Betty said as she stood to hug her favorite grandson and kissed him on the cheek.

"Hello beautiful." Loco greeted as he held on to his grandmother's hand. "How have you been, G-Ma?" he took a seat next to her.

"I'm good child. What brings you by?" she looked at him curiously.

Loco cleared his throat and gazed at his two little girls. "Mama, I need you to look after the girls for a while."

"I thought…" she stopped in mid-sentence and shook her head. "I'm getting up in age. I don't know if I can be running after these babies."

"G-Ma," Melanie interjected, "we aren't babies any more. I promise you wont even know we're here."

"Right, we will basically take care of ourselves. You know that." Mahogany nodded.

G-Ma looked at them and sighed, "Well I guess it won't be no harm. Loco, these girls are still your responsibility, hear?"

He nodded and touched the top of her hand. "Yes ma'am. I know."

After he left the girls with his grandmother for the next time, Loco made it a point to visit whenever he had the chance. He wanted them to know that he still loved him, but his lifestyle wouldn't let him be the father they deserved. He sent money via Western Union every week he wasn't around and they were the fliest girls at school. Even with their father miles away, the girls still had evil lurking in their hearts.

"Ring, Ring Ring..." Nadine's house phone rang she rushed from outside to answer it.

"Hello." She said out of breath from her sprint to the phone.

"Heyy cuz, you ok?" Trish inquired hearing Nadine struggle catch her breath.

"Yea girl, I was changing my room around when you called. What's going on? You going with us to Cali, right?

"I sure am, I have my money for my plane ticket just packing now and about ready to head your way." Trish replied with a wide grin she was anxious to take this trip considering she needed to get out of the area for a little rest and relaxation.

An Uneasy Truth 2

"Great, I can't wait I've never been to Cali before." Nadine said as she sat on the couch and flipped through a magazine that lay nearby.

"This is going to be so much fun." Trish said as she poured herself a glass of lemonade.

"True indeed, but let me finish this room come on over about six o'clock tomorrow evening.

"Okay see you then." Trish said before disconnecting the call.

Nadine ran back up the stairs to finish rearranging her room, she was excited about the trip to Cali and couldn't wait until Thursday. "It's the Cali trip count downnnn." She sang to herself as she danced around her room.

"What is going on in here?" Paula asked looking around Nadine's room at furniture in disarray.

"Oh, hey mama I'm changing my room around I need a new view." Nadine said as she slid her nightstand to the other side of the room.

"I see, well do you need help?" Paula offered as she stepped inside Nadine's room.

"No mommy I got it, thank you." Nadine said as she continued moving about.

"Ok have you packed yet?"

"That is my next mission, one thing at a time mommy on thing at a time." Nadine said with a smile still pushing around her bedroom furniture.

"Okay I'll be on the porch if you need me." Paula said as she stepped back out and headed downstairs.

Nadine continued moving things around until she got them exactly how she wanted them and then she began to pack the small things she would need in her suitcase. After she was done she gathered her necessities for the shower and headed down the hall to the bathroom. As she walked passed the steps she could hear her mother outside laughing and joking with her cousin Karla.

"Oooo that woman irritates my soul." Nadine said to herself as she continued to the bathroom.

Paula and Karla sat sipping wine coolers and talking on her porch for an hour.

"Cuz I'm gonna run up to the lady's room." Karla said as she stood to walk inside.

"Oh, go on ahead baby. Heyy Mrs. Shepherd!" Paula said as she spoke to her Neighbor across the street. Karla went on inside and headed up the stairs instead of the bathroom she made a B line to Paula's bedroom. Nadine could hear footsteps in the hall while she laid across her bed reading she laid the book down and just listened because that was odd her mom usually let her know she was back in the house. She tip toed to her door and cracked it she could see Karla rummaging through her mom's belongings in her room.

"What the fuck are you doing?" Nadine said through gritted teeth as she watched Karla slide the tennis bracelet her father had given her mom years ago into her pocket.

An Uneasy Truth 2

"Little girl you better get the fuck out of my face." Karla said in a menacing tone as she pushed pass Nadine.

"Fuck no ain't no get out your face you fucking thief!" Nadine shouted as she hit the steps on Karla's heels. It was no fucking way she was going to get away with walking into their home and stealing from her mother.

"Whooa what's going on?" Paula asked in confusion as she stepped into the house, their yelling and cussing was getting loud and completely out of character for Nadine.

"Mama this bitch just walked in your room and stole your bracelet." Nadine accused angrily.

"I don't know what this child is talking about, Paula. But what I do know is I'm not gonna be another bitch out your mouth" Karla said denying she took anything.

"Dump your pockets, then. I watched you put it in your damn pocket." Nadine yelled

"Well cuz?" Paula said as she shifted on one foot and placed a hand on her hip.

"Fuck both of y'all." Karla said as she attempted to leave.

"BITCH FUCK YOU!" Nadine yelled as she quickly snatched Karla back by her tight fro and rain blows on her. "ALL…"

Pop!

"THE…"

Pop!

"SHIT..."

Pop!

"MY MAMA DO FOR..."

Pop!

"YOU."

Pop!

Nadine was in a rage as she spoke and popped the shit out of Karla with her fist.

"Wait stop, baby." Paula said as she pulled Nadine off Karla who was now knotted up from the punches Nadine dropped on her. Nadine stopped swinging and took off upstairs she was beyond heated she hadn't had to put hands on any female since the sixth grade when she classmate picked on her.

Paula helped Karla off the floor. "Thanks, cuz." Karla said as she gathered her footing.

"Nah how you thank me is dump your pockets." Paula said in a calm tone.

"Now Paula you know I would never." Karla began but was cut short when Paula raised her hand to silence her.

"Either you will dump them and prove Nadine wrong or I'm going in your fucking pockets my damn self." Paula said in a simple and plain tone.

"Paula." Karla said in defeat she knew she had the bracelet in her pocket either way it was going to be exposed

An Uneasy Truth 2

whether she removed it, or Paula did. She knew Paula was a woman of her word but decided to test the waters anyway.

"I didn't steal from you Paula. That's my word." Karla said as she slowly started toward the door.

Paula beat her to the door and stuck her hands in Karla's pocket when she felt the bracelet she pulled it out and held it up. She stuck it in her pocket and reached for the door knob as if she was going to open it and quickly backhanded Karla sending her flying into the steps she never saw it coming. Then she walked over and stood over her, "Get the fuck up and get out of my house you are no longer welcome." Paula said in a calm tone she felt no need to continue to beat on her considering Nadine had just given her the ass kicking of her life. Karla talked tough but couldn't bust a pea in a food fight.

Karla got up and left as asked with no words she knew she had fucked up, so she took her battered and bruised walk of shame as the neighbors stood around outside watching as she walked to her car shaking their heads they had already heard most of the commotion.

Paula locked her door and went to check on Nadine who was sound asleep. She laughed to herself as she replayed that workout she had just laid on Karla she knew she didn't care for her, but this explains why. Paula figured she wouldn't even discuss it with Nadine and just let it die she was going to Cali and she wanted nothing but her to enjoy herself.

Ring ring, ring ring

"Hello." Nadine answered

"Good morning beautiful." Loco greeted her voice brought a smile across his face.

"Hey now. I'm so excited about this trip, I can't wait to see you." Nadine cooed. She was so happy to hear from Loco and would be even happier once she got in his presence.

"Are you sure you wanna come?" Loco joked he was excited too, he couldn't wait to introduce Melanie and Mahogany to her.

"Of course, I do." Nadine was almost offended until she heard him laughing.

"Are you all packed? I can't wait to see you." Loco said as he stood looking out the window at the girls playing in the yard.

"Not quite but I will be before we leave. I think you called to make sure I'm coming." Nadine said with a smiled in her voice.

"Well Miss Smarty pants I miss you and wanted to hear your voice." Loco said laughing to himself because she was only half right yes, he did wanna make sure she was still coming but he was missing her.

"Aww Lo. I'm coming." Nadine cooed

"Good because I'm sending for you tonight, I don't wanna wait until tomorrow." Loco said

An Uneasy Truth 2

"Aww shit Lo okay I gotta finish packing, bye." Nadine hung up and ran upstairs to finish packing.

Ring ring, ring ring

"Hello." Nadine answered out if breath She couldn't believe she just had to sprint back down stairs for the phone again and she was trying to rush pack.

"Hey Baby. Everything ok?" Paula said hearing Nadine out of breath.

"Hey mommy, yes I'm just trying to pack. We're leaving tonight instead of tomorrow." Nadine replied with a bit of frustration.

"Oh yeah I'm aware Loco called last night and spoke with me about that when you were sleep unfortunately I got called in before you got up this morning. That's what I was calling you for and since I'll be working a double I won't be home to see y'all off." Paula explained

"Dang mommy. Ok." Nadine said as she processed what her mom had just said.

"I left you some money and I love you be safe and call me once y'all land ok I gotta go." Paula rushed off the phone.

Nadine hung up and hurry up and dialed Trish who picked up on the third ring.

"Hello"

"Trish, we leaving tonight. Come over here."

"Ok Be there shortly.

Nadine disconnected and jetted up the stairs just as she reached the top the phone rang again.

"Damn it!" she shouted as she jogged back down stairs to get the phone.

"Helloo." She answered with irritation.

"Don't pack nothing unless you feel it's necessary I'm taking you shopping, see you later." Loco said before hanging up.

Nadine hung up and plopped down on the couch. "He could've said that shit when he called the first-time shit." She said to herself.

A few hours later....

Pam, Trish and Nadine danced around the living room all excited to be headed to Cali.

"Ok. what time is it?" Pam asked as took a sip of her soda.

"4:30." Trish replied

"Ok Let me call Smurf to drop us off at the airport." Pam said as she dialed Smurf on the telephone.

Nadine and Trish moved all their bags to the front door.

"Ok he's on his way." Pam said as she went up the stairs to the bathroom.

About ten minutes later Smurf blew his horn for the ladies to come outside.

"Oh, you not carrying bags?" Nadine joked

"You know I got y'all." Smurf said as he made his way up the stairs to grab a few bags and take them to the car. Trish pulled the remainder of the bags on the porch while Nadine locked up.

They climbed into Smurf's car and headed to the airport on their way to Cali.

Loco got the call they boarded their flight, he timed the flight to the minute as they exited the terminal he stood there waiting patiently. When his eyes laid on Nadine his heart raced he watched as she smiled and looked around in excitement. When her eyes met his she ran straight to him and jumped into his arms she couldn't believe she was in California it was all new to her since she hadn't been outside of D.C, Maryland or Virginia.

"Hey you." Loco greeted as he lifted her to his lips kissing her passionately.

"And you will have plenty of time for that. Let's Go!" Pam said as she temporarily broke up their reunion. Trish laughed as she followed behind Pam, while Nadine and Loco slow strolled out to the car.

"Aye cuz how you figure what I'm driving?" Loco asked noticing Pam walked to his car out of all these cars in the parking lot and choosing correctly at that.

"You are my cousin nothing else needs to be said." She replied as she helped drop their luggage in the trunk.

Everyone climbed inside and he headed straight to his grandmother's place.

"Loco this is my cousin Trish, Trish this is my baby Loco." Nadine introduced the two.

"Welcome to Cali cuz." Loco greeted

"Hey now. Thank you. What you got planned?" Trish asked anxious to get out and meet new people.

"First we gonna sit down this luggage and then we gonna hit the mall. You with that?" Loco asked looking back in the rearview mirror at Trish.

"I'm with it, this y'all town I'm just a visitor." She replied with a smile and sat back in her seat to enjoy the ride.

"G-ma Betty know I'm here?" Pam asked Loco

"Yup and I'm having Leo dropped off at G-ma Betty as well." Loco replied he knew Pam's main reason for coming to Cali was to see her son Leo who was being raised by his father Jermaine who stayed in Cali.

Pam's heart calmed down a bit knowing her cousin had taken care of things with her ex Jermaine who she wasn't trying to have any contact with.

As they pulled up to G-ma Betty's house and parked Nadine took in the atmosphere. Pam jumped out and ran up to the porch and bust through the door.

"G-ma I'm home!" she shouted as she took off toward her room like a big kid.

"Oh Pam!" G-ma said as she embraced her with a warm loving hug planting big kisses on her forehead, she hadn't seen her in over a year and was very glad to have her home. Pam was the youngest of her grandchildren and the wildest. G-ma Betty was secretly hoping Pam was either here to stay and raise her son or take him with her and slow down.

"G-ma did Jermaine come by yet? Pam asked anxiously she couldn't wait to see Leo and how much he had grown.

"Oh, cuz I told him I would call on the way back from the mall." Loco chimed in.

"Oh, okay groovy that gives me a chance to pick him up some stuff while we there." Pam said as she helped bring the remainder of their luggage inside G-ma Betty's house.

"Oh, my who are these two pretty young ladies?" G-ma Betty asked noticing she had company.

"I'm sorry G-ma, this is my lady friend Nadine and her cousin Trish. Ladies this is G-ma Betty the glue of my heart.

"Aww thanks grandson. Hello, ladies nice to meet you. Make yourselves at home." G-ma Betty said as she embraced them both with a hug and shuffled down the hall to the kitchen.

"Walk with me out back baby." Loco said as he pulled Nadine by her hand toward the back door.

Mahogany and Melanie were in the backyard with their new dolls and dollhouse Loco had bought for them. The girls continued to play acting as if they hadn't heard Loco enter the yard and just as he thought he was creeping up on them Mahogany quickly turned around and sprayed him with her water gun.

"Oooh shit!" Loco laughed being caught off guard.

"Gotchu daddy." Mahogany laughed she was tickled.

"Oh yea, I gotchu little girl." Loco laughed as he rushed closer and began to tickle Mahogany.

"O nahhh you know it's not going like that daddy." Melanie yelled playfully as she jumped on Loco's back and rain playful punches on his head.

Nadine stood entertained, she had never seen this side of Loco but she loved it.

"Okay okay hold on y'all. Let me introduce y'all to somebody." Loco said between laughing and tussling with the girls.

"Say you quit!" Melanie giggled as she pulled out her little water pistol as Mahogany sat her entire body on top of Loco's chest. Loco was laughing so hard he couldn't get a word out. Nadine sat on a patio chair nearby laughing at the three they were so cute. Finally, Loco was able to peel the twins off him and get up off the ground.

"Come over here girls." Loco said as he took a seat next to Nadine.

"Yes daddy." They said in unison as they walked close.

"I want y'all to meet my lady friend Nadine, Nadine this is Melanie and Mahogany my 10-year-old twins." Loco smiled proudly.

An Uneasy Truth 2

"Hey pretty ladies it's nice to meet you both. How do I tell y'all apart?" Nadine asked with a warm smile. The twins sensed her energy and smiled back they liked her already she radiated positive warm motherly energy.

"Hi. I'm Mahogany." The first twin with a set of long pigtails with orange ribbon on each one said as she hugged her.

"And I'm Melanie." The second one who wore the same pigtails but with a pink ribbon on each said as she leaned in and hugged Nadine as well.

"And I like orange and she likes pink that's how you tell us apart. We gonna finish playing now." Mahogany said as she grabbed Melanie's hand they kissed Loco's cheek and ran over to continue playing with their dollhouse.

"Woooow Lo, you are a dad?" Nadine asked in awe.

"Yeah they are everything to me. My best kept secret you know?" Loco said sincerely.

"Yea I understand, they are special to you I see."

"And so are you that's why I brought you out here and introduced you to the most important women in my life. Because you too are now a very important woman in my life." Loco said sincerely as he looked into Nadine's eyes. She could feel the tears welling up in her eyes.

"Lo. Damn that's deep." She said as she leaned in and softly kissed his lips.

"Ooooooooooooooo…" Melanie teased.

Loco and Nadine burst into laughter. Before getting up to head to the mall.

"We'll be back shortly girls, behave." Loco said as he stepped into the house.

"Okaaay. we always do." Mahogany sassed jokingly.

"Yup daddy." Melanie cosigned as she sat the dolls on top of the house in a complete row.

Once Loco had left eyes sight they began to use the dolls as target practice with their water pistols as they always did.

"We need BB guns." Mahogany suggested.

"Where you hear about that?" Melanie inquired she had never heard of BB guns.

"Daddy!!" Mahogany yelled as she took off through the house trying to catch Loco. Loco and the girls had just climbed into the car.

"What's wrong Ma-ma?" Loco asked as he stepped back out the car seeing her running out the house.

"Can you bring us BB guns back please?" Mahogany asked in a pitiful tone with sadness in her eyes, she knew this worked on Loco every time. Loco was puzzled by her request but the look she was laying on him was getting to him.

"Anything for you Ma-ma, now go back inside and lock the door." Loco said as he kissed her on the cheek and sent her back inside.

An Uneasy Truth 2

He got in the car and they were off to the mall. They shopped for hours, Pam picked up items for her son Leo she couldn't wait to see how big he got she had called his dads mom before they left just to be accurate on his size it made her feel kind of weird being his mom and not really knowing the basics about him but she knew the reasoning's, Loco grabbed the girls BB guns he Wasn't quite sure why BB guns of all things but it was whatever for his girls meanwhile Trish and, Nadine shopped for outfits. Everyone got what they needed Loco paid and then they headed to the car. After piling all that would fit in the trunk they squeezed a few bags between Trish and Pam and headed back to G-ma Betty's house.

Just as they were walking through the door the smell of home cooked food smacked them and lead them all to the kitchen. G-ma Betty stood stirring a pot of red beans and rice that was cooking on the stove while Mahogany flipped frying pork chops right beside her and Melanie at the far end of the counter pouring sugar in a large pitcher of tea with lemons.

"Y'all should probably put y'all bags down first." Melanie said with a giggle. They all looked down noticing they were all still carrying shopping bags an erupt of laughter began, once everything was sat down they went back into the kitchen and sat around the large dining table.

"Ummm daddy." Mahogany crept up and whispered in Loco's ear while everyone was engaged in conversation.

"Yes Ma-ma." He replied with a grin as he wrapped bone arm around her little waist already knowing what she wanted but decided to play along.

"Did you happen to get what we asked for?" she whispered in his ear.

"Yea daddy." Melanie chimed in softly in his other ear. Loco couldn't help but to laugh at the twins they moved like they were on a shake down.

"Of course, I did, I'll give 'em to y'all after dinner." Loco said in a hushed tone.

"Okay" they said in unison before hurrying over to get the dinner plates out.

"Dinner is served. Now y'all know I'm too old to be serving folks so help yourself." G-ma Betty said as she took a seat at the table. She was feeling tired, but it warmed her heart to have family together with no problems and drama loving one another.

Nadine was enjoying the dinner G-ma Betty and the twins had prepared of fried pork chops, homemade mashed potatoes with gravy, steamed cabbage, red beans and rice and homemade buttermilk biscuits. She and Trish were feeling right at home.

"Oh, Lo I gotta call mama, I was supposed to call her when we landed it completely slipped my mind." Nadine said shaking her head

"Oh, baby the telephone is hanging right there, or you can go in the front room. You gotta let ya' mama know you're safe, child." G-ma Betty said as she showed Nadine where the telephones were.

Nadine thanked G-ma Betty and called her mom at work since she didn't get an answer at home, she let her know she was safe and how much she was enjoying herself before having to rush off the phone due to Paula having to get back to work. There was a soft tap at the door as she went to join the others back in the kitchen, so she let Pam know so that she could answer the door.

Pam walked over and peeped out the little window aside the door once she saw it was her baby boy she snatched the door open a grabbed him up in the biggest hug.

"Hey little man, mommy has missed you dreadfully." Pam squealed as she hugged on Leo who was now 2 years old. He just smiled and hugged her back, it was like looking into a mirror for Pam she couldn't believe how much he looked like her.

"Leooooo!!" The twins shouted in delight as they headed in his direction, he jumped out Pam's lap and took off to them. The twins kissed and hugged all over him they loved their little cousin Leo.

"Awwww Pam this little man is what you left behind?" Nadine asked as she sat next to her best friend and hugged her. Deep inside she couldn't believe Pam kept a secret like this from her but was glad to know and happy to see what truly brought her joy. Trish sat on the love seat with G-ma Betty just engulfed in the love it truly put her in a happy place.

Loco stood in the doorway of the kitchen admiring this beautiful moment, he was happy Pam was happy. He looked over at Jermaine with a slight head nod signaling he could dismiss himself now. He never liked Jermaine but gave him his respect because he was a stand-up dude taking care of business when Pam fell short

Jermaine understood that was his cue to leave. "Alright I'm gone. See you later Leo, I love you." He said as he hugged his son before leaving.

Pam rolled her eyes, what he didn't know was he wasn't going to see him later because he was leaving for D.C in a week with her. No one knew Pam's plans and wouldn't until it was time to board the plane.

"You hungry Leo?" Mahogany asked her little cousin seeing that he kept looking toward the kitchen.

"Yes." He shouted as he jumped up from Melanie's lap and grabbed Mahogany's hand and all three headed to the kitchen. Pam followed behind.

"You girls are really growing up. But here's a little tip from cousin Pam don't do it too fast, y'all hear me?" she said to them as she fixed Leo a small plate.

"Yes." They replied in unison. What they didn't know was Pam saw the doll line up out the window before they were about to leave for the store, she also heard the BB gun request and lastly, she saw her cousin buy the BB guns as requested at the store. She intended to find out what her little cousins were up to and nip it in the bud.

Once Leo was done eating the twins cleared the table and washed the dishes, Leo sat on the floor playing with the blocks Pam had bought him earlier at the mall.

"Here you go girls." Pam said entering the kitchen with the two BB guns one for Mahogany and one for Melanie. They both looked at each other with an evil smirk.

"Line 'em up Mel." Mahogany said as they both ran out the back door to the doll house.

An Uneasy Truth 2

Pam watched from the window as Melanie lined up the dolls and Mahogany loaded the BB guns she was amazed they moved swiftly. They each took turns shooting the dolls off the house until they got tired. As they were walking inside Pam stopped them in the kitchen.

"That's what y'all wanted them pistols for?" she asked through squinted eyes.

"Well yeah, the water guns don't have no power. Come on Melanie let's get ready for bed." Mahogany replied before they walked through the kitchen headed for the bedroom upstairs.

"Y'all going to get ready for bed?" G-ma Betty asked as they hit the stairs running.

"Yesss.." they replied in unison as they went into their bedroom and gathered their pajamas and shower necessities.

"Imma get in first." Melanie said as she grabbed her stuff and ran in the bathroom before Mahogany could object.

"Dang." Mahogany said as she plopped down on the bed and waited. She sat on her bed and admired her BB gun. "I wish this was real, I would shoot mama ass." She thought to herself as she replayed all the physical and verbal abuse Michelle inflicted on her.

"I'm out Ma-ma." Melanie said snapping Mahogany out her thoughts.

"Oh ok." She said as she jumped up and went to get in the shower.

They both suffered abuse at the hands of their mother Michelle, so they shared the same feelings toward her. Mahogany more than Melanie because she suffered the bulk of it being the oldest of the twins by two minutes.

"Cousin Pam!" Melanie shouted down the stairs.

"Yeesss!" Pam replied she wasn't sure who she was replying to seeing Melanie had removed her ribbons from her hair and was now wearing an old pair of stockings with the legs cut off tied in a knot on top of her head.

"Is Leo staying over here tonight?" Melanie asked

"Yess." Pam replied

"Okay well send him up to bathe 'cause its bedtime." Melanie said almost sounding like an adult.

"You heard the baby." G-ma Betty said giggling as she ushered Leo toward Pam.

Pam gathered his Pajamas she bought him and took him upstairs.

"We got it from here." The twins said as one grabbed his hand and the other his towel, wash cloth, and pajamas. "Oh, Pam we gonna put a diaper on him tonight for him to sleep in." Mahogany said.

"No, you not I go pee-pee." Leo interjected

"Leo, you are not about to pee on me tonight." Mahogany said with her little hands on her hips.

"You not gonna pee on me girl. I pee myself." Leo said as he stormed away and into the bathroom at waited at the tub.

An Uneasy Truth 2

"Looks like y'all gotta problem." Pam said as she tried to creep away.

"Oh no cousin you do 'cause if he don't wear this diaper he sleeping with you, hope you ready for bed 'cause its bedtime." Mahogany said walking into the bathroom and shutting the door. Melanie followed behind her and laughed the entire time. She had already figured he was gonna sleep with his mom anyway.

Pam made her way downstairs laughing at what had just transpired, everyone downstairs heard everything and were too laughing heartily.

The night went on after the children went to bed, G-ma Betty was still sitting around laughing and talking with Loco, Trish and Nadine. Paula took a walk out back to smoke. After a while G-ma Betty had gone up to bed and everyone was sitting out back with Pam. Loco offered them all wine coolers and Nadine declined.

After a while they all grew tired, Loc showed Trish to the spare room while Pam took camp on the pull-out sofa and he and Nadine headed to the basement. His grandmother always kept it reserved for him. Set up with a King-sized bed and loveseat and the walls were filled with family pictures the basement gave studio apartment vibe. Nadine was so tired she took her shoes off and climbed right into the bed. Loco walked over and sat her luggage near the dresser and then began to remover her clothes from all the shopping bags before getting comfortable himself. He climbed in the bed and held Nadine as if she would slip away at any moment and drifted off to sleep.

The week seemed like it flew by it was now the day before their flight back home, Trish was skeptical about leaving she was digging the Cali life after being introduced to a few of Pam's cousins and their homeboys. Nadine wasn't ready to leave she was enjoying everything about her trip especially Loco, the twins and Leo. The twins were loving Nadine they even let her braid their hair which shocked G-ma Betty because she had to fight with them to do two pigtails. Loco was loving every second of the time spent with his favorite ladies he regretted having to stay in Cali a bit longer or even letting Nadine go back to D.C he knew it wasn't good to be moving the twins around, but he didn't wanna leave them behind either, He was a young man with heavy decisions he needed to make.

"I gotta just enjoy it while it last." He thought to himself as he hugged Nadine while she watched the girls play with Leo in the backyard.

"Lo, run to the store for me baby." G-ma Betty called out from the kitchen.

"Yes ma'am. You wanna ride baby?" Loco asked Nadine.

"Sure." Nadine replied

"And we wanna go too." Melanie said as she, Mahogany and Leo walked into the kitchen for something to drink.

"Ok let's go then." Loco said as walked over to get the list G-ma Betty was holding, he pecked her in the cheek and they left to go to the store.

The kids sang all the way to the store while Nadine coached them on. Loco laughed at them all being silly and

An Uneasy Truth 2

having fun. Once they arrived he parked and they all got out to go in, they were so busy enjoying each other they never saw Michelle lurking feet away.

Loco was collecting the items on the list while Nadine pushed the shopping cart with Mahogany to the left of her and Melanie on her right both wearing their little pocketbooks across their chest while Leo rode laughing and tossing stuff out the cart.

"Oh, isn't this cute." Michelle said with a menacing glare as she stood at the end of the aisle.

Loco shook his head from side to side he couldn't believe out of all the times and all the places Michelle could be she is here right now and about to be on some bullshit.

"Michelle I'm not doing this with you." Loco said as he dropped the bottle of honey in the cart and ushered his crew past Michelle.

"Oh, but we are. Mel and Ma-ma so y'all just gonna walk pass your mama like I'm nobody huh?" she said as she stepped in front of the cart causing Nadine to stop.

The twins glared at her through squinted eyes they hadn't forgot what she said and did nor would they forgive her for the years of abuse.

"Ok you done making a scene?" Loco asked as they maneuvered around her and continued to walk through the grocery store while onlookers stared.

"Nope she gonna finish it for me." Michelle said as she snatched Nadine by her ponytail to the floor, in the moment Nadine hit the floor she bounced up like a ball giving Michelle no time to react. She kicked her directly in her knee breaking her leg clean and hit her with a two piece before she hit the floor. Loco didn't even have a chance to react Nadine moved so fast.

"Bitch I don't know you nor do you know me, you better fix your leg." Nadine said in an angry tone as she stormed off with the twin on her heels and Leo in the shopping cart Loco jogged to catch up.

"We should probably leave I'm not trying to go to jail in Cali." Nadine began to panic.

"Take the kids to the car I'll be out in a second." Loco said as he moved quickly to the clear checkout and paid for the items before quickly moving to the exit. As he was leaving a paramedic rushed in to assist Michelle somewhere in the back.

Loco got in the car and peeled off. There wasn't any time to wait around to see if Michelle would press charges. Mahogany sat quietly and partially satisfied, She was happy to see Michelle get beat down to the floor like she did to he on numerous occasions.

"Y'all ok?" Loco asked noticing they both had been very quiet the entire ride.

"Yeah daddy we ok. Right Ma-ma?" Melanie said nudging Mahogany. Loco looked directly into Mahogany's eyes through the rearview mirror. He sensed something uneasy about her but decided to let it go for now.

"Yeah daddy we okay." Mahogany said as she held Leo tight in her arms.

An Uneasy Truth 2

Nadine didn't say a word she rode in complete silence, she couldn't believe this was the second ass kicking she had to hand out in the last two weeks. She was completely enjoying her trip until that moment. Loco grabbed her hand and held it until they reach the G-ma Betty's house. He could feel the heat radiating off her as she stared straight ahead into space.

"Mel take Leo inside to G-ma Betty, Mahogany grab the two smallest bags and I'll bring in the rest. We'll be inside in a minute." Loco said as he turned off the car and waited for the girls to do as he asked. Once they were inside he directed his attention to Nadine gently turning her face toward his.

"I want to apologize for that situation back at the store, I would never put you in harm's way intentionally." Loco said with deep sympathy in his eyes. He really felt fucked up about her having to physically defend herself because of him.

"Lo, you know I don't even know what to say. I had to beat on my mother's cousin for stealing and lying now I got your twins mom tryna take my head off. I don't want to, but we should probably leave tonight. I don't want no drama at your grandmother's house." Nadine said now sad she knew the drama wasn't her own, yet she knew this situation with Michelle wasn't over.

"Hey hey now, the girls just told us what happened. Nadine are you okay?" Pam asked as she opened the door and pulled Nadine out and into a hug.

Loco sat there stuck on her wanting to leave. He didn't want her to go but he understood her reasoning he never expected this shit would happen and he wasn't going to force her to stay. He got out of his car and carried the remainder of the bags inside while she and Pam talked.

"Baby is what the twins are saying true?" G-ma Betty asked as she stood in the doorway with one hand on her hip.

"Unfortunately, G-ma it is." He replied as he sat the groceries on the table took a seat dropping his face in his hands.

"You really care for her I see." G-ma Betty said in a comforting tone as she walked over and laid her hand on his shoulder.

"More than I've ever cared for anyone." Loco admitted.

"Come talk to me upstairs." G-ma Betty said as she slowly headed for the stairs.

"Okay G-ma, let me make sure Nadine is okay and I'll be right up." Loco said as he got up to walk outside to where Trish, Pam and Nadine stood talking.

"Gimme your keys Lo." Pam demanded before he could get a word out.

"Hold on Pam." Loco said with furrowed brows.

"Nahh Lo we need to step off." Trish said as she stood at the rear passenger door.

Loco looked over at Nadine who was very nonchalant. "Just gimme the keys." Pam said as she snatched them out his hand and jumped in the driver seat and pulled off. Loco stood there confused and hoping his gangster ass cousin Pam didn't make things worst.

"Let her go baby, trust me you want her to cool off." G-ma Betty said through her open bedroom window. She sat in her recliner and waited for Loco to come upstairs she was about to drop a jewel on her young grandson. Loco tapped on the door before entering and took a seat in a recliner across from G-ma Betty and listened as she schooled him.

Pam, Nadine and Trish rode around for hours just talking and listening to music. Nadine didn't wanna discuss the day's events she just wanted to free her mind.

"You good cuz?" Trish asked from the backseat.

"I'm good, lets head back." Nadine said as she reclined the passenger seat. While Trish sat stretched across the backseat.

"As you wish." Pam said as she maneuvered Locos car through the California streets and back to G-ma Betty's house. They got out and walked around the side of the house to the backyard, Pam grabbed her weed stash and rolled up a joint.

"Let me hit that." Nadine said in a nonchalant tone as if she was a smoker knowing she had never smoked a day in her life. Pam asked no questions she passed the joint to Nadine, Trish sat wide eyed in shock this was very surprising and the chain of events had been unpredictable, so she didn't bother objecting either.

Nadine took a long pull of the joint and started coughing and choking instantly after she calmed down a bit she hit it again long and hard and passed it back to Pam this time she didn't choke or cough and blew the smoke out with ease. She leaned back in the patio chair and stared at the sky.

"Awwww yeaa. you feel that? This that good Cali shit." Pam said as she passed the joint to Trish. Nadine was on a wave she could feel the high creeping throughout her body it was weird and confusing at the same time.

"Trish, she high." Pam said as she grabbed the joint from Trish who was trying to pass it to Nadine however Nadine was riding the wave in full relax mode.

"Yup..." Trish laughed as got up to go inside.

"I think I'mma call it a night, too. Come on, Nadine." Pam said as she tapped Nadine before getting up to walk inside. Nadine didn't say a word she was high as gas and wrapped in her own thoughts. Once they entered the house Nadine went downstairs showered and climbed in the bed Loco wasn't far behind, after he showered he climbed into the bed and held Nadine. Nadine rolled over and kissed him passionately she knew what happened wasn't Loco's fault and despite the events she didn't want to leave on bad terms. Loco kissed her as her gently caressed up and down her back turning her on with his touch They made love until day broke.

"Lolo." Leo called out innocently as he pulled on Loco's arm trying to wake him up. Loco thought he was dreaming until he rolled over and Leo was right there smiling at him with his big bright brown eyes.

An Uneasy Truth 2

"Hey man you ok?" Loco said as he sat up on the bed.

"Come come." Was all Leo said before his little legs took off up the stairs. Loco grabbed his boxers and a pair of Dickie's that laid on the loveseat nearby and went upstairs to see what Leo wanted him to see. As he reached the top of the basement stairs he could hear a female and male arguing he picked up his pace and followed the voices that lead him to the porch where Pam and Jermaine were in a heated argument in the street Melanie, Mahogany and Leo stood at the door of the porch listening and watching.

"Ma-ma take them upstairs to y'all room." Loco said as he pushed them all toward the stairs inside the house, he didn't know what this was about but what he did know was it could get ugly instantly. He saw Trish struggling to hold Pam back, Pam wasn't an argumentative person she was with the action.

"Hey now what's going on?" Loco asked as he walked between Trish and Jermaine.

"Loco talk to your cousin she is trying to take Leo back to D.C with her." Jermaine said pointing in Pam's direction before he began to paced back and forth in the street rubbing the sides of his head. Loco pulled Pam away from everyone and spoke to her through gritted teeth.

"What are you thinking about?"

"I want my son Lo, he's mine too. I have the right it's been two years." Pam tried to explain as she broke down crying. Loco knew at that moment he really couldn't talk her out of leaving without Leo. True she lived a wild life, but she has made him the center of whatever she has done since she got him when she got to Cali.

"You right cuz you are his mother I just hope you making the right decision because you pulling him out of structure to take him across the country." Loco said sincerely still giving her the real.

"I understand. But I'm ready to raise my son." Pam said as she wiped the tears from her face meaning every word. Loco nodded and walked back over to Jermaine who had stopped pacing and was now smoking a cigarette leaning on the side of his car.

"Go ahead and pull off Jermaine, he leaving with Pam." Loco said as he stuck his hands in his pockets. He felt bad for Jermaine.

"What?! That's bullshit Lo and you know it." Jermaine shouted as he climbed inside his car, he knew that Loco wasn't to be played with or one to repeat himself if he said pull off it was for his best interest, so he did cursing Pam his entire ride home.

As Pam, Trish and Loco were walking up the stairs a car bent their corner with screeching tires causing all three to turn around and see what was going on it stopped in front of G-ma Betty's house three girls hopped out Michelle's older sister Tiny who was far from it in fact she was huge 6 feet 325 pounds, Michelle's younger sister Kyla who was 5 foot 3 160 pounds and Michelle with a battered face who had to be assisted out the car on crutches.

"Where that bitch of yours at?" Michelle yelled at Loco

An Uneasy Truth 2

"Ha! From the looks of things that's not somebody you really wanna see again." Pam antagonizes.

"Michelle y'all need to get back in that little ass car and go back home, that shit is dead." Loco said as he turned to walk up the stairs.

"The fuck you think u..." Michelle began but was cut short when Pam slapped her to the ground and started punching the biggest sister in the face. Trish quickly jumped in effect as she jumped on top of the big one who was struggling to get up off the ground pinning her arms to the ground with her knees and beating her bloody. Neighbors were now in their windows watching the brawl.

"Oh Shit!!!" Loco said as he rushed over to try to break up the brawl. He was having no luck until suddenly...

"POW POW POW." Three shots rang off and the brawl split up, Michelle and her crew jumped in the car and peeled off. While Loco, Trish and Pam scrambled for cover behind nearby cars

G-ma Betty quietly walked back inside and put her pistol away. The three walked back inside relieved no one was hit and neither Trish or Pam had a scratch on them.

"Aww man did you see G-man betty she said POW POW POW!" Mahogany explained in excitement as she reenacted how G-ma Betty moved and grabbed her pistol and fired shots in the sky. Melanie and Leo fell out laughing.

"G-ma Betty where you get that from?" Pam asked shocked to know that not only did G-ma Betty had a pistol she was busting it.

"I got what I need, and I use it if need be child and that's all you need to know." G-ma Betty said with a smirk as she went to the kitchen to cook a nice lunch before the girls and Leo left to board the airplane. Pam went and packed up she and Leo's belongings while lunch was being prepared, while Loco, Nadine and Trish hung out in the living room laughing at the twins who were now reenacting the grocery store scene between Nadine and Michelle for Trish.

After everyone sat down said grace and ate they loaded the luggage into Loco's car said a prayer and their goodbyes.

"I'll be back to D.C as soon as I can." Loco told Nadine as he hugged her tight. Nadine struggled with her tears this goodbye felt so final.

"Okay I'll call as soon as I get home." Nadine said before kissing him and leaving to board the airplane.

Seven months later...

Nadine stood in her bedroom mirror rubbing her now small round belly. Should couldn't believe she was about to be a little person's mother. When she got home she told her mother all about her trip from meeting Locos 10-year-old daughters to whipping their mama in the store Paula was shocked and intrigued it made her love Loco even more. Nadine and Loco spoke often though she never mentioned her pregnancy due to him going through enough

An Uneasy Truth 2

with the passing of G-ma Betty she even swore Paula to secrecy not to tell Loco she was pregnant, and Paula held her word every time she spoke to him when he called. Pam had been true to her word with Leo wherever she went he went and she never put him in harm's way, she and Leo went back to Cali before she started showing after G-ma Betty passed so she had no idea of her pregnancy either.

Ring, ring ring

"Hello." Nadine answered as she sat down on the couch with a bowl of chocolate ice cream.

"Hey, how are my babies?" Paula asked

"We're good mommy, just sat down from cleaning my room." Nadine replied

"Okay I'm just checking on y'all, I'll be home shortly. I love you." Paula said

"Okay mommy. See you in a few, love you too." Nadine said before hanging up.

Paula was very surprised to know she was about to be a grandmother, it was very unexpected, but she accepted it whole heartedly true Nadine was her only child and she wanted the best however she was a bright young woman with a good head on her shoulders she knew she would be an excellent mom besides she had Paula who would be with her every step of the way.

Two months went by and the last time Nadine spoke with Loco he and the twins had moved to Texas. She had seen Markel on numerous occasions here and there they even held conversation from time to time. He even asked if the baby she was carrying was his, but every time it came up she would end the conversation and go about her way the truth was she wasn't sure. Paula automatically assumed it was Loco's; unaware of the encounter that occurred between Markel and Nadine. Nadine was within days of her due date and scared as hell. On June 17th Isis Renee Monroe was born. Paula was ecstatic.

It was a warm September day when the doorbell rang, Nadine put the bottle she was making Isis down and went to answer the door. When she looked out the peephole she saw Loco she felt like her knees would buckle instantly. She pulled herself together the second time he rang the doorbell and opened the door.

His eyes fell on Isis as the door opened and his heart melted he knew she was his as soon as he laid eyes on her, Smurf had called him months ago and told him Nadine had a baby bump.

"Hey Lo." Nadine said sweetly as she stepped to the side and allowed Loco, Mahogany and Melanie in the house. Loco was in awe, he couldn't take his eyes off Isis. He took in every inch of her, kissed and smelled her. He knew she was his because she had the exact same birthmark he and both the twins had on her left calf. The twins' eyes lit up when they saw their little sister Loco reached for her and Nadine handed her to him without hesitation Isis even calmed her fussing.

"What's her name?" Melanie asked as she played with Isis hand.

"Isis." Nadine replied

An Uneasy Truth 2

"Ooo that's so cute just like her." Mahogany said as she reached over and picked Isis up out of Loco's arms and sat next to Melanie.

"Nadine let me talk to you a minute please." Loco said as he raised up and grabbed Nadine's hand and led her to the porch.

"She's mine. And You should have told me." Loco said in a disappointed tone.

"Lo, you got enough going on." Nadine said as she shifted on one foot feeling uneasy how could she tell someone she loved so much her baby may not even be his. He too had no clue what had transpired between she and Markel.

"How are you so sure she is yours?" Nadine asked innocently.

"You can't tell me she not." Loco said through clenched teeth, unknowingly to her he was aware of what happened between she and Markel due to him running his mouth in the neighborhood, but he knew in his heart Isis belonged to him.

"I'm not doing this with you Lo." Nadine said as she got up to go back inside Loco grabbed her arm pulling her into his arms.

"I love you and I love Isis, we can avoid this as long as you like but you forever straight. I get it." Loco said in a calm tone before passionately kissing Nadine's lips. They walked back inside where they spent a few hours together while Nadine cooked.

"Oh well hello…" Paula said in a surprised voice she had just gotten home from work to Melanie and Mahogany playing on the couch with Isis.

"Hiii." They said in unison

She moved swiftly toward the kitchen she couldn't wait to see Loco she missed him just as much as Nadine, she thought he was good for Nadine he was a standup guy in her eyes.

"Loooooooooo!!!" she yelled as she ran up and hugged him.

"Hey mama Paula." He replied with a smile hugging her back. She was a genuine woman and he loved her she birthed the love of his life. They all sat and had dinner while chatting about what had been going on in their lives. Loco sat cradling a sleeping Isis just staring into her face he could see his nose, chin, and lips there was no doubt in his mind that she was his. Nadine watched Loco looking at Isis and her heart felt full in her gut she knew he was right but what was the point he was leaving to go back to Texas in a few hours, so she decided it would be what it was life goes on. Paula was so happy and in the moment, she felt bad about keeping this precious information from Loco, but her loyalty was to her daughter.

"I love you." Loco whisper in a sleeping Isis ear as he laid her in her crib, he walked downstairs said goodbye to Paula and gathered the twins after putting them in the car he walked back to the stairs where Nadine stood suppressing her tears.

"We're headed back to Texas tonight. I love you and whatever y'all need it's done." Loco said as he wrapped his arms around Nadine pulling her close inhaling her scent.

"Why do these goodbyes feel like goodbye forever?" Nadine asked as tears threaten to fall from her eyes.

"It's never forever. I'm always around even when I'm not." He said as he pulled her face to his and kissed her.

"I love you too Lo. Call me when y'all make it to Texas." Nadine could no longer hold the tears she loved this man Loco wiped her tears and kissed her face.

"My lifeline Nadine you have that Don't cry baby and your number will be the first I dial." He said referring to Isis as he reached in his pocket and handed her twelve crisp folded one hundred dollar bills then he got in the car and he and the twins were gone.

Nadine walked inside went to her room and broke down this was a situation she never thought she would be in nor did she expected all these emotions after having the baby. She cried herself to sleep that night. Paula went to sit on the porch and enjoy the night air as she sat sipping on her wine cooler a car drove by slow past her house she noticed it was Markel and made a mental note to keep her eye out for his lurking ass she was all for Loco and the last thing she needed was him to pop back up in Nadine's Life.

Ring ring, ring ring"

"Helloooo" Paula sang into the telephone.

"Heyy mama Paula, Its Pam." Pam greeted trying to talk over Paula's music.

"Oh heyy baby hold on let me turn this down." Paula said as she sat Isis in her swing and turned down the music.

"Heyyy Pam I'm back, how are you and Leo?" Paula asked excited to hear from Pam it had been awhile since she had been around.

"We are just fine, Is Nadine around?" Pam replied

"Yea sure baby." Paula said before calling for Nadine.

"Hey Pam." Nadine said she was happy to hear from her best friend she needed to talk to her it had been months since she spoke to her she was glad she called.

"Hey Hey, how are you and baby girl?" Pam asked

"We're good, you gotta come see her she's getting so big and fast." Nadine smiled as she looked over at Isis.

"Unfortunately, it won't be soon. I'm in Texas Loco got locked up." Pam said in a sad tone.

"Fuck! Where are the twins?" Nadine yelled as she plopped down on the couch startling Isis Paula came out and picked her up to calm her down.

"Michelle has them." Pam said regretfully.

"Damn this is fucked up. Now what?" Nadine said.

"I don't know, but the more info I get I will call and give you." Pam said she felt fucked up for having to call and tell Nadine about this.

"Ok girl thanks." Nadine said before hanging up. She got up and went to put on her shoes she came back downstairs and headed for the door.

"Where you going baby?" Paula asked

"For a walk." Nadine said before closing the door behind her. She started walking down the block just taking in the night air she needed to clear her mind this was all a lot to take in. As she walked a car drove slow beside her she was lost in her thought not paying any attention.

"Excuse me can you give me directions?" the male voice asked

"Where you trying to go?" Nadine asked bending down to see Markel was the driver.

"Wherever you wanna go." Markel said with a sly grin. Nadine thought what the hell could it hurt she just needed to getaway for a minute and climbed in the car.

As time went by and Loco slowly faded to the background while Markel was now her light once again, they had become an item against Paula's wishes. Nadine soon moved out and was pregnant again with Shell. Two years had gone by with no word from Loco just random envelopes in her mother's mailbox every week addressed to Isis Monroe some envelopes even came with cute little notes for Isis from Loco. Nadine wasn't sure where he was or how the twins were but what she did know was he kept true to his word.

Present day*

Valerie clutched her stomach as her morning's breakfast spilled on the ground behind the dumpster. After all the years she had worked for Smurf's company, she couldn't believe what she had just seen. It would be the hardest pill she had to swallow. *How am I ever going to be able to tell my son that his father is dead?*

She loved Vee. She had loved him since she was 14 years old. And when he was released from jail on good behavior she was there to pick him up. She walked to the corner, she flagged down a taxi. She needed to get far away from there. Once she was inside the taxi, she gave him her address and leaned her head against the headrest of the backseat. Her mind was going a mile a minute. Every time she closed her eyes, all she could see was Vee's lifeless eyes. She had never been weak to moving dead bodies but seeing the love of her life sprawled out on the floor was a bit much to handle and getting to her.

"Ma'am." The cab driver looked at her through the rearview mirror. "Hello... Miss, we have arrived," the taxi driver said in a snappy tone as he tried for the second time to get Valerie's attention.

"I'm sorry, how much do I owe you sir?" she asked snapping out of her daze.

"$10.75 ma'am." He replied

She dug into her pocket and handed him $12 and climbed out of the cab and damn near got smacked by a truck as she crossed the parking lot. She didn't care she just kept walking as the driver blew his horn at her.

"Hey Val!" a female greeted from a distance. Valerie just waved and continued walking into her building. She didn't wanna be rude, however, seeing Vee, her love and the father of her son, with a bullet hole in the back of his head had her head elsewhere.

"Hey mommy, you're home early," VJ greeted with a confused look on his face. He knew when his mom worked she would usually return home in the wee hours of the morning. He walked into the kitchen to make himself a turkey and cheese sandwich.

"Hey baby. Yea, I'm not feeling too great. I'll be in my room if you need me," Valerie said as she moved swiftly toward her bedroom. She was feeling like with just one glance at Vaughn Jr. she would break down. When she made it to her room, she quickly locked the door and slid to the floor and cried. She cried long and hard, silently until she fell asleep. She slept for hours curled up in fetal position right in front of her bedroom door.

VJ sensed something weird about his mom when she walked through the door. After her not coming out of her room or responding to his knocks, he just left her alone.

Dang, what did I do? he thought to himself as he walked back into his bedroom for the sixth time. He flopped down on his bed and threw his pillow on his face. With a dad that he adored even though he was in and out of his life and a mother constantly on the move with work, he began to feel ignored.

Today he found out that he'd made the honor roll for the third quarter straight with no one to share it with. He said a small prayer that his aunt Destiny taught him before she moved out and cried himself to sleep.

The next morning VJ got up, showered, and got dressed for school. On his way out, he looked down the hall and noticed his mom's door still closed so he figured he wouldn't bother her. He grabbed his things for school and headed to his bus stop.

I hope she not acting all funny when I get home, he thought to himself as he boarded the school bus and took a seat. He rode to school in deep thought, not enjoying his morning like all the other kids that were laughing and talking on the bus around him.

An Uneasy Truth 2

Chapter 4
Destiny

Destiny stood in her full-length mirror admiring her slim frame in her pink and purple boy short panty set. She was in love with herself, standing at 5 feet 6 with one hundred and sixty-five pounds, proportioned perfectly. She was glad she took after the women on her daddy's side of the family all of them were shaped like coke bottles with curvy physiques and not her mama's side "They are shaped like pears, all pears." She laughed to herself as she continued to get dressed. Her cell phone began to vibrate on her dresser. She walked over and saw it was a text from Summore's right hand, Allure.

Sup girly, you fuckin wit me tonight? -Allure

Destiny smirked. She didn't think they would make it so easy to get on with them, but they did. The night Isis pulled Destiny to the side, Allure was lurking. She watched them talk and go their separate ways, A few days later she went at Destiny.

"Soooooo Destiny, there's this party coming up and we need a third girl, you interested?" Allure asked as she took a seat next to her at the bar. It was closing time and the club was basically empty besides the 2 or 3 girls still talking and giggling amongst themselves as they head towards the exit.

"Yeah sure. I'm always down to get dollars," Destiny said.

"That's what I'm talkin' bout. Gimme your number and I'll be in touch," Allure said as she handed Destiny her cell phone for her to type in her number. Allure's intentions were to interfere with whatever Isis had going on, however, what she didn't know was she just made it easier for Isis' protégé's plan to go smoother than she could imagine. Not only had she begun to block Summore money flow at the club, she was about to get a few extra perks at Allure and Summore's expense of course.

Yup, I sure am. Meet you at the club. Destiny texted back.

Destiny got dressed and walked into her kitchen, grabbed a bottle of water, and plopped down on the loveseat that sat in front of her balcony and gazed out the window. She sat thinking about her family and how she missed her big brother, Supreme, who was serving time on a drug and a gun charge, while her big sister Valerie lived not too far away but they had no real relationship. She didn't let that interfere with her bond with VJ though. She loved her nephew to pieces and spoke to him often. She made a note to call him later when she thought he was home from school. Her mother was a faint memory considering Supreme raised she and Valerie both. Their mother was a resident of the street and a slave to the pipe. She worshipped everything above them; she'd left the three while they were youths to fend for themselves. Supreme took odd jobs cutting grass and helping elderly neighbors and sold drugs to keep the bills paid, food in the fridge, and clean clothes on them all until four years ago when he got locked up.

Destiny looked around her small, one-bedroom apartment and she could honestly say she was doing well on her own. After Supreme got locked up, Valerie and Destiny got into a big fight and she tossed a seventeen-year-old Destiny and her belongings out on the curb. As Destiny gathered her belongings, she promised herself she would never go back, and she worked her ass off at the club for everything she had. She walked over to the little desk that sat in the corner of her living room and sat down. She was gonna write her brother today since she hadn't written him in a few weeks. In all her letters, she made things seem as though they were good, but she'd had enough of what was going on with Valerie and it was time she let him know.

After writing her letter, she sat and re-read it then balled it up. She then wrote the same letter excluded anything about Valerie. She figured all that could be saved for the visit she planned to make to see him. Supreme didn't play about either of his sisters, but Destiny was the baby and very dear to him. He loved Valerie and she loved him too, but he and Destiny had a deeper bond. Destiny looked at the calendar that hung above her desk and put a circle on the Wednesday after next to remind herself of when she could expect a response and could plan her visit to Ohio to see her brother. Destiny got up to turn on some music to kill her sadness. She heard a tap on the door, she walked over and peeped out the peephole to see her nephew. She opened the door and saw the sad expression on his face.

"VJ what's wrong?" Destiny asked as she pulled him into her embrace.

"Auntie I made honor roll again for the third quarter, just wanted to share it with somebody." VJ replied as he cried into his aunt's chest.

"Awwww baby that's great. I'm so proud of you, let's celebrate we going to get something to eat put your backpack in the bedroom." Destiny said as she wiped his tears and sent him on to the room. She grabbed her shoes and put them on before grabbing her keys and wristlet and heading to the door where VJ stood waiting. She drove to Jaspers in Largo and parked. They went inside and had a great meal she didn't know what had him down when he arrived but she was glad she could take his mind off it for a while. Once they were done eating and talking they left and got back inside Destiny's car.

"VJ I'm going to swing by your moms and grab some clothes for you, you can stay with me a week or so." Destiny told VJ as she pulled into traffic.

"Okay auntie." VJ said as he sat back in the passenger seat and stared out the window. He wondered if his mom knew or even cared where he was.

As if Destiny had been reading his mind she said with a warm smile "And don't worry about your mom I'll talk to her."

An Uneasy Truth 2

Chapter 5
Valerie

"Boom, Boom, Boom, Boom." The sound of someone banging on Valerie's door like the police woke her from her tear provoked sleep.

"Whaaaaaaaaaaat?!?!" she yelled as she stumbled a little on her way. She was still a little out of it from the sleeping pills she had taken to sleep all day.

"If you don't open this muthafuck'n door you gon' know what," Ali yelled from the other side of the door. He had been banging on the door for over an hour. Not to mention, this was his 5th time coming by and this time he wasn't leaving until he saw that she and his godson were ok.. He and Valerie had been best friends since they were in eighth grade, so he knew her well and knew this wasn't like her. Something was up.

After shaking off the groggy feeling the sleeping pills were giving her, she made it to the door and peeped out the peephole. She swung the door open wide enough for Ali to walk inside and then walked back over to her sofa and stretched out across it.

"Ali, why the fuck is you banging on this damn door like the police?" Valerie asked as she threw one of the blankets she had on the sofa over her face.

"What the fuck you mean, why am I banging like the police? I haven't heard from you in two weeks and every time I've been by I haven't been getting an answer until today. Do you even know where VJ is?" Ali ranted noticing VJ wasn't around, then snatched the blanket off her face as he waited for her response.

Tears immediately filled Valerie's eyes, she had been so deep in her own funk that she had neglected VJ. Truth was, she had no clue where her son was on this beautiful Friday evening. The last time she could say she saw him moving, breathing, and speaking was almost a week ago when she witnessed his father's dead body.

Ali saw the look on her face and shook his head, and watched the tears rolling from the corner of her eye and puddle in her ears. Something was going on with his best friend and whatever it was, it was taking her out of her character. It wasn't like Valerie to mistreat or neglect her son. She'd been putting him first since the day she found out he was coming into the world.

Valerie sat up on the sofa, placed her elbows on her knees, and sobbed. Not only was the man she loved dead, but she was losing her son as well. She was clearly depressed she felt hopeless, weak even. "Ali, I don't know where VJ is. I've been so caught up in my own emotions that I've been ignoring and avoiding him. I can't look at him. I keep breaking down." Valerie said through her tears.

Ali was confused. He looked at her, waiting for her to elaborate on what could make her neglect such a good kid. "What's going on Val?" Ali asked with sincerity and concern as he took a seat next to her and hugged her.

An Uneasy Truth 2

"Vee is dead." She replied as she cried.

What Valerie had just said had totally took him by surprise and was very unexpected, Ali knew Vee from the streets as the terminator, no matter what the nigga Vee went through he came out unscathed. "Damn that's fucked up but not unexpected seeing that the nigga was a loose cannon." He thought to himself. "That's why you can't look at VJ? Because Vee is dead?" Ali release his hug around Valerie as he grabbed her shoulders making her face him as he looked at her through squinted eyes.

"You don't understand Ali," Valerie began to explain but was quickly cut short.

"What about VJ though? Have you stepped out of your emotions to tell him his father is dead?" Ali asked he was beginning get pissed at Valerie's selfishness.

"I didn't know how," Valerie said as she buried her head into the pillow and sobbed uncontrollably.

Keys jingled in the door, it unlocked, and opened. In walked VJ with Destiny right behind him. Destiny and Valerie hadn't spoken since Valerie put her out. Their eyes met, and Valerie instantly went off.

"The fuck is you doing here?" Valerie yelled as she jumped up off the sofa and headed Destiny's way. Ali immediately stepped in the middle. He had no clue what the riff was, but he wasn't about to let Valerie's unstable ass bust a move.

Destiny stood at the door, unbothered. She was used to Valerie's hateful attitude toward her. Anybody that would put their 16-year-old sister out on the street for no good reason has no heart or maybe she just didn't have one for Destiny.

"Are your serious right now? VJ go ahead and get your things." Destiny expressed as she directed VJ toward his room. VJ didn't wanna leave the room but his auntie said move so he did.

"Oh, hell nahh, he not going nowhere," Valerie shouted with spittle flying from her mouth as she struggled to get at Destiny.

"Wait Val. You just told me you ain't know where he was, why wouldn't you want him to be with your sister; someone who clearly has the time and mental stability to care for him right now?" Ali asked as he turned Valerie to look him in the face.

"Fuck dat Ali!! I don't give a fuck what you talking about and fuck her!" Valerie yelled as she slipped by Ali and slapped fire outta Destiny. Destiny instantly went into action as she tagged Valerie with every blow. Valerie lost her footing, causing her to fall to the floor. She hadn't expected Destiny to throw blows and certainly not with the power she had behind each blow, causing Valerie's mouth and nose to leak blood. Ali didn't even expect the speedy pop off. He had to admit Destiny was trained to go the way she was beating his best friend down.

"Whoa whoa whoa lil mama." Ali said as he grabbed Destiny and swung her in the opposite direction of Valerie to prevent her from landing anymore blows. Valerie was now on her feet and with the program. Those punches sobered her up real fast. Just as Ali turned the opposite way, she snatched Destiny through his arms by her feet causing her to slam into the hardwood floor.

An Uneasy Truth 2

"Oh Shit!" Ali yelled once he realized what had just happen but by the time he turned around Valerie and Destiny were fighting on the floor.

"Mama nooooooo!" VJ shouted as he walked into the living room and witnessed his auntie and mom fighting and tussling on the floor.

Damn, Ali thought to himself as he broke the two apart, winded and outta breath he looked at the two Valerie battered and bloody and Destiny with her hair all over her head and a few scratches on her neck.

"Now that that's out of y'all system..." Ali said as he fell against the wall out of breath like this was his fight.

"Auntie let's just go." VJ said as he walked up to his auntie and grabbed her hand pulling her to her feet.

"Fuck No!" Valerie yelled attempting to attack Destiny again, but Ali stepped in her path.

"Fuck you Val! On everything, you gonna regret putting your hands on me. I ain't come here for this. My nephew came to me and what I won't do is turn my back on him when he needs me. Now Let's go VJ." Destiny said as she held VJ's hand and headed for the door.

VJ let go of Destiny's hand and walked over to his mother who was now sobbing as she made eye contact with him. "Mama, I love you," he said before kissing Valerie and walking back over to Destiny taking her hand. Valerie broke down sobbing uncontrollably. Ali walked Destiny out to her car, she hit the automatic lock, and VJ got inside the back seat.

"What the hell is going on with y'all?" Ali asked in concern.

"That bitch hates me. Always has and always will. But that's a story she has to tell you because I've never done her foul." Destiny replied with tears welling up in her eyes.

"That's fucked up. It's more to it though." Ali said as he embraced Destiny in a warm hug.

"I guess so but thanks." Destiny said as she broke the embrace and climbed into her car.

"Hey, lock me in, hit me if you or my man back there needs anything." Ali said giving VJ a head nod.

Destiny punched his number into her cellphone and hit save said goodbye and pulled off she had no intentions on ever hitting Ali up she knew his rep but did appreciate his concern. She couldn't believe she literally had to fight her older sister. Destiny rode with the radio playing. She was lost in her thoughts the entire drive back to her apartment. She parked and turned off the car and glanced back to tell VJ they were home, but he was asleep.

"Hey sleepy head were home." She said as she gently shook his leg.

"I'm so tired auntie," VJ said as he unbuckled his seatbelt.

"I know baby." Destiny said as she got out and walked around to assist him out the car and into the apartment building.

An Uneasy Truth 2

"Auntie, what was all that about back at my mama's house?" VJ asked innocently as they made their way into Destiny's apartment.

"Nephew, go get comfortable. No need to worry yourself with grown up problems, that's what you got me for." Destiny said sweetly as she kissed VJ motherly on the cheek and sent him on his way down the hall. VJ did as he was told and prepared for bed. Destiny went into her kitchen and pour herself a glass of wine. Her mind was still circling around why after all these years Valerie would have the balls to lay hands on her.

That's all good. I let dat ass know I'm a force all by myself the way I taxed it, Destiny giggled to herself as she took a seat on the loveseat in her living room. She grabbed her cellphone and dialed up Isis. She hadn't spoken to her since the night she approached her. The phone rang three times before she answered.

"Hey D. What's up?" Isis answered trying to multi-task in her kitchen while holding her phone between her cheek and shoulder. She was glad Destiny called because she was kind of anxious to know how "Operation: Road Block" was coming along.

"You. I'm just calling to check in, you busy?" Destiny inquired.

"Cooking' up some dinner. What's going on witchu?" Isis said stirring the stir fry that cooked on the stove.

"Crazy shit. But about that thing, it's in motion." Destiny said in a cool tone as she broke down the Dutch she was splitting and dumped the guts.

"Ahhhhh music to my ears considering what my life has been like since I've seen you last." Isis said with a smile while making plates. "C'mon in here hard heads!" Isis yelled to Lem, Sky, and Jamier

"Ooooo I see you got your hands full," Destiny joked hearing the three arguing over who was going to sit where.

"Girl yes. Let's do lunch tomorrow around 1. Send me your address and I'll pick you up," Isis said.

"Oh, ok cool. I have my nephew with me is that okay?" Destiny asked as she inhaled the weed smoke deeply.

"Yeah that's fine. I guess it's a play date," Isis laughed.

"Sounds fun to me, sending the address in a few. See you tomorrow," Destiny said as she disconnected the call.

"I'm not sitting in no damn corner!" Sky roared. Isis head snapped around so fast she damn near caught whiplash.

"Ooooooooooo...." Jamier and Lem said in unison

"What's wrong with your mouth?" Isis asked with one hand on her hip and the other ready to smack fire from Sky's ass. Sky stood there with no reply pouting.

"Goodnight Sky," Isis said before letting her temper get the best of her.

"BUT I ain't eat yet," Sky whined.

"Oh, you got words now?" Isis asked sarcastically. "Ha! GOOOODNIIGHT!" she demanded while pointing toward her room. Isis wasn't having it, but she wasn't about to let the weight on her shoulders reflect in negative actions towards her children.

"Lem take this plate next door for me please," Isis said handing Lem a plate wrapped in aluminum foil to take to Troy.

Lem walked next door and tapped on the door, he waited a few seconds before knocking a second time as he was knocking Troy opened the door. "Sup lil man," he greeted as he allowed Lem inside. Lem walked over and placed the plate on Troy's dining table.

"Oh nothing, my mama asked me to bring you this. How you feeling?" Lem replied as he and Troy took a seat on the sofa.

"Aw I'm good lil' man thanks for asking. How are you? Your mom told me about the recent chain of events," Troy inquired in a concerned fatherly tone.

"I did what needed to be done so we peaceful now you know?" Lem said making full eye contact with Troy. Troy understood fully. He had to respect the young man he saw his mama hurting and got rid of the pain. What no one knew was that Troy too killed his mother's boyfriend for abusing his mother as well he beat him to death with his bare hands he spent a little time in juvenile detention.

"True," Troy said in a somber tone because he knew Lem killing his father would forever change his life. "Why your mama ain't bring this over here anyway?" Troy inquired.

"Oh, she dealing with Sky and her mouth." Lem laughed

"I see. Check this out though, if you need to talk about anything I'm here and tell your mom I said thanks and come see me later," Troy said as he walked Lem to the door and dapped him up.

"Ok, thanks Troy," Lem said as he went back to his apartment.

"Mama, Troy said come see him later," Lem said with a laugh as he warmed up his plate in the microwave.

"Oooooooooo…." Jamier teased.

"Oooooo my ass. Boy eat and go to bed both of you it's already late," Isis fussed.

"Yes ma'am," the boys said in unison as they dug into the teriyaki chicken and steak with stir fry vegetables over white rice.

"Mommy, can I eat now?" Sky asked pitifully peeping her head around the wall of the kitchen.

"Get your plate Sky, and I better not hear your voice no more tonight," Isis said as she sat the warm plate on the counter for Sky. She had already begun to warm it up in preparation to call her but as always, it was like she was in sync with Isis and just knew when to appear. Isis

An Uneasy Truth 2

laughed to herself as she wiped down the counter tops, *That's crazy.*

After the kids were all fed and down for bed, Isis walked out the front door and began to lock it behind her but was startled by Troy.

"You can lock it for safety but you and I both know they safe," Troy said wrapping Isis in his embrace.

Damn this feels good, Isis thought to herself as she inhaled his scent.

"I'm glad to see you okay," she said, touching the bandage that peeped through his wife beater looking into his eyes. There was a moment of silence before Troy grabbed her hand and led her inside his apartment. Isis noticed his facial expression had hardened a bit as she took a seat on the loveseat.

"You want a drink?" Troy asked as He walked into the kitchen and poured himself a glass of Hennessy and Coke.

"Sure, but are you even supposed to have that?" Isis asked with a sly smirk.

"It's been weeks so I'm good. Thanks, mom," Troy joked as he handed her a glass of Hennessy and coke.

"So, word on the street is the lil' bitch Summore and some nigga that use to frequent the club y'all work at had something to do with me getting crowned unconscious and shit I don't know the dudes name as of yet but I'm working on it but I do definitely know Summore is behind it," Troy said, making Isis almost choke on her drink with that unexpected news.

Isis swallowed her drink and replayed what Troy had just said several times in her head.

"You're fucking wit me, right?" Isis asked with a confused look on her face. Sure she had plans for her but none ever involved physical harm to anyone.

"Nope, I kind of wish I was. Now she has to be handled," Troy said as he took a shot of Hennessy to the head.

"Nahh I got this Troy. She put my children in danger and could've killed you," Isis said as she began to pace the floor.

"You stay clean. You got enough to deal with concerning lil' man and all," Troy said as he grabbed Isis' arm to stop her from pacing the floor.

"I gotta go. I have an early day tomorrow. Thanks for the drink," Isis said as she headed for the door. Troy reached it steps before her stopping her from opening it.

"That's cool, but don't you worry about Summore. She's taken care of. I care too much for you and your kids to have not already handled it," Troy said as he lifted her chin until Isis lips met his and kissed her passionately. Her knees had damn near buckled; there was so much passion in his kiss. She had never had a kiss so intense, so she welcomed it. The kiss was getting deep. Troy lifted Isis and she wrapped her legs around his waist.

"Damn," She panted.

An Uneasy Truth 2

"All I could think about was you and the kids when I was laid in that hospital," Troy said as he placed kisses along her neck to her ear. Isis could feel his manhood swelling in his basketball shorts. The intensity of him kissing her and up and down her neck and his rod sitting perfectly between her pussy lips through her panties, she was ready to go.

"I want you," Isis whispered in his ear. The Hennessy, lack of sex, and the heat and chemistry between them had her ready to jump on him and ride to ecstasy. Troy embraced her tightly and carried her to his bedroom with her legs still wrapped tightly around him. He gently laid her on his bed. He lifted her dress and slowly removed her panties that were soaked with her juices. Isis laid back on her elbows watching his every move. It turned her on how gentle he was. Troy leaned in and began to kiss her while swift and smoothly removing her 38C cup breasts that sat full and perky in her bra. "Damn he unhooked dat like a pro, yessss." She thought to herself as He began to plant soft kisses along her neck and chest until he reached her nipples. Isis laid back in bliss. Every touch felt so good. Troy then trailed kisses down her belly until he was eye level with her kitty, then he began to study her like science as he licked her throbbing love button. "Ooooo oooooo Ahhhhh Oooo…" Isis sounded off with every stroke of his tongue. His skills were causing her to squirm and moan with delight as she gripped his head, the pillow and anything in her grasp. Troy was fully enjoying the taste and effect before he standing up and dropping his shorts. Isis watched with a smile anticipating his entry as she rubbed her clit.

Troy began to rip open the rubber to roll it on, but Isis stopped him before he could roll it on she got on her knees on the bed and took him into her mouth. She was quick and swift, yet gentle Troy didn't even see it coming. His eyes began to roll back as Isis slobbered and slurped up and down his thick wood.

"Mmmmmmm," she moaned with her mouth full as Troy began to finger her tight, soaking wet pussy. Isis stopped and climbed to the top of the bed Troy followed. She then laid on her back and spread her legs and Troy climbed between them, neither thinking of the rubber. Troy eased himself into her inch by inch as she adjusted to his size and began to grind back.

"Oooooo shiiiittt.," Troy moaned as he and Isis' body collided in a rhythmic sync. The rhythm of their skin slapping was turning Isis on even more she could've sworn the room went pitch black and the moon and stars appeared. She was in heaven with every thrust.

"Yessss oooooo yessss…" Isis moaned digging her nails in Troy's back as she pulled him deeper into her.

They met and matched each others climax for two hours before passing out in each other arms.

Bom Bom Bom Bom.. Troy's alarm blared.

"Oh my God, what time is it?" Isis jumped up and looked at the clock it read 5:50am.

"I'm sorry. I wake up at the crack of dawn. Let me turn it off so you can get a few minutes more of rest," Troy said as he reached over next to him on the nightstand and turned off the alarm clock.

An Uneasy Truth 2

"No no no no. I gotta go. I'm taking the kids out today," Isis said as she grabbed her items of clothing and quickly put them on. Troy watched as she put her clothing on, admiring every curve and the mean mug she had on her face as she rushed like she wasn't going just next door. It was turning him on all over again.

"I'll lock the door behind myself, thanks," Isis said as she kissed him on the lips and rushed next door.

Troy laughed to himself as he thought about their unexpected yet completely satisfying night.

Isis crept into her apartment quietly, trying not to wake the kids.

"Oh nahh mama. What u doin'?" Sky asked in a whispered tone as she flipped on the kitchen light as if she'd just caught her child creeping in after curfew.

Isis burst out into laughter. *This kid is too much,* she thought to herself. "Oh nahh, little girl. What you doing up?" Isis asked with her hands on her hips.

"Let's start with my questions first seeing that you the one creeping in the house at almost 6 o'clock a.m. with your yesterday clothes on," Sky said as she pointed to the clock on the microwave.

"Let's make breakfast," Isis said, avoiding her daughter's question because clearly that was none of her business.

"Oh let's avoid questions too huh mama? I'll help you though," Sky said as she hopped down off the stool and started to gather the sausage and eggs from the refrigerator.

Isis laughed to herself because clearly her daughter was every ounce of her child. She could recall a similar scenario when she was younger catching Nadine creeping in the house just as Sky did on this morning.

After cooking breakfast Isis stood in her closet and realized she didn't really wanna get dressed and kind of wanted to just lounge around today so she got on the phone and call Destiny telling her they would just have a game day at her apartment instead of going out. Destiny was cool with that she didn't feel much like going out either her body was achy from her fight with Valerie. After a few hours Destiny and VJ knocked on Isis' door.

"Heyy y'all, come on in." Isis greeted as she opened the door and hugged Destiny.

"Heyy everyone." Destiny said as she spoke to all the kids.

"Lem, Sky, & Jamier this is my friend Destiny and her nephew VJ." Isis introduced everyone.

"Hi." VJ said to the other kids and Isis.

"Ok ok now that that's out the way y'all go pick out some games and get to know each other." Isis said as she sent the kids to the bedroom.

"You thirsty girl?" Isis asked as she grabbed herself a glass out the cabinet to pour a Hennessy and coke.

"Yeah sure." Destiny said as she took a seat at the dining table.

"Now tell how things are going." Isis said as she sat their glasses on the table and took a seat across from

Destiny. Destiny pulled out a pre rolled Backwood of white widow and sparked it.

"Oh hell yea." Isis said with glee as she grabbed the incents and lit one.

"I Gotta move tonight with them hoes, I been diggin' in Summore's pocket since you gave me the green light speaking of which I got something for you." Destiny said as inhaled the smoke and she retrieved a large thick folded yellow envelope and handed it to Isis.

"Well damn..." Isis said as she started thumbing through the bills.

"Yeah and we not done." Destiny laughed

"Well little mama the task just got a lil' thicker, she tried to put my seeds in danger so we goin' way further than fucking with her money now." Isis said as she took a sip of her drink, Destiny just sat back and listened to the next move Isis was breaking down for her as they smoked.

"What you say your name was?" Sky said looking at VJ as he played the video game with Lem. She just couldn't take her eyes off him there was something about him that made her uneasy.

"VJ. Why what's up with you? Why you keep looking at me like that?" He replied as he quickly turned to look at her.

"You look like a bad memory that's all." Sky said with her face scrunched up before getting up off Lem's bed and walking out of the bedroom and down the hall to the living room where Isis and Destiny were. Jamier busted out in laughter it tickled him how Sky never knew what to say out her mouth.

"What's her problem?" VJ asked as they continued to play the video game.

"That's just her." Lem glanced over and laughed.

Sky walked into the living room just as Isis and Destiny were ending their smoke session and conversation.

"What's up baby girl you ok?" Isis asked noticing the stank look on Sky's face.

"Can I go outside? It ain't nothing but boys in there." She replied

"As a matter of fact, go get dressed we going to get our nails done and stick Troy with the boys. She went to call Troy and let him know the boys were coming over for a bit he gladly agreed.

"Yesss! OK!" Sky shouted as she ran to her room and got dressed.

"Hell yea I could use a fill in." Destiny said looking at her gel nails.

Isis was in the process of gathering snacks for the boys when her cellphone vibrated so hard it almost fell off the kitchen countertop before catching it just in time.

"Hey girlie what's up." Isis said seeing it was her girl Cita.

"Heyyy What's up with you? You haven't been to the club and you took a leave from school." Cita asked she was concerned about her friend she hadn't heard from her since she rushed out of the party the night Troy was attacked.

"Soooo much, I'mma swing by the club next week. I'll fill you in on everything as soon as we meet up." Isis replied

"Okay and don't forget. Oh yeah be safe out here." Cita said before disconnecting the call.

Isis took the boys over to Troy who was happy to have them then She, Sky and Destiny headed out to the nail shop. They had a good outing and even grabbed some Popeye's on the way back. While they were standing in the Popeyes line a pretty curvy older woman tapped Isis on the shoulder.

"Excuse me don't I know you." Pam said innocently. Isis turned around to see her cousin Pam standing there looking just as young as she did when Isis was a kid. She hadn't seen her since before Mel was born, Pam pulled her in for a strong warm hug.

"Oh my god Pam? How have you been? How's Leo?" Isis said smiling as she stepped back to look at her cousin. Her mom always referred to Pam as Nadine's cousin and best friend when they went through pictures and spoke of Pam growing up. After Loco was locked up Pam and Leo left Texas and moved to North Carolina with family but still calling every now and again.

"Everyone is good, I've been great I moved back to the area to work. I'm staying with Uncle Key in Northwest." Smurf told me you're into fashion now. Are you still in school?" Pam asked as they moved up in line. Smurf being Loco and Pam's blood cousin always kept tabs on Nadine and Isis and reported back to Loco.

"Woow that's awesome, Yeah I'm still in school for fashion design. Give me you contact info." Isis smiled as she passed Pam her cellphone to enter her info.

"Is this my little cousin?" Pam ask admiring Sky. Sky had her grandfather Loco's eye color and was the splitting of her image of her mother.

"Yes, that's my baby girl. And this is my home girl Destiny. Excuse my manners I'm so damn rude." Isis laughed at herself.

"Hi." They both said

"Cousin I will definitely be in contact okay." Isis said she hugged Pam and stepped up to the register to order their food.

"OK cuz. See y'all and tell your mama call me." Pam said as she went on her way out to her buddy's car. That made her day to see her family because unfortunately she hadn't seen them in a long time.

"I see your mood changed." He said seeing the big smile on Pam's face as she got into the car. She had been in a sad mood all day until now.

"I just saw my cousin in there I haven't seen her in years that's all. It was good to see her and good to meet her daughter that's all." Pam said as she buckled her seatbelt.

"Awwww I'm glad that changed your mood." He said as he pulled out of the parking lot into traffic.

An Uneasy Truth 2

Pam rode in her thoughts for a while as she replayed Isis pretty face in her head, "Damn she looks like Lo."

Isis, Destiny and Sky arrived back home to all the guys waiting at the table for the food.

"Jahmier is this why you said text you when we pulling up so y'all could be sitting at the table?" Sky asked snappily.

"Of course, girl we hungry." Jahmier replied as he walked over and grabbed one of the bags out of her hand.

"Of course, girl we hungry." Jahmier replied as he walked over and grabbed one of the bags out of her hand. They all burst into laughter at the two and began to break down the food, make plates and eat.

Isis looked around with a slight smile as she watched all the kids, Troy and Destiny laugh, talk and eat. "It has definitely been a good day." She said to herself.

Chapter 6
Summore

Summore sat in the dressing room of Club Spread feeling like she was on foreign territory, she was now at a new club in the DMV and she was starting from the bottom since all her outfits were mysteriously shredded and none of her other clients were fucking with her to even rebuild her funds to come out of her slump. Her plan with Black to take out Troy went up in flames even Black wanted to kill her at this point. She had recruited him one night he came to the club to see Isis.

"Oh, she was at home playing house with Troy." She slurred off her drunk tongue unknowingly making Black furious inside, but he played it cool fucked Summore and got more information on Troy. She called him to hook up and laid the plan on him and he was with it anything to have Isis to himself

"What you looking all down for? It's time to get this money." Allure said as she walked in with Destiny behind her.

"But of course." Summore said as she perked up a bit and laced up the straps of her heels up her calf.

"Hey Summore." Destiny greeted with a smirk.

"Let's get this money." Summore said as she sashayed pass Destiny bumping her on purpose she didn't care for her and as far as she was concerned her recent bad luck didn't begin until she started hanging around. Destiny didn't give two shits how

An Uneasy Truth 2

Summore felt about her she was there to apply pressure and from Summore's demeanor she was doing just that.

 Pharrell & Ludacris' "Shake your money maker" was blaring through the speakers as the three walked onto the floor, it was people everywhere true to her girl Cherry's word the club was definitely popping. Destiny, Allure and Summore went their separate ways as they worked the floor, Destiny thought she was tripping when a set of twins dressed in see thru black jumpsuits with bodies to die for sat down at a table near the black of the club in the corner not far from the bar. "They are really pretty." Destiny thought to herself as she sashayed through the club headed to the bar.

A waitress walked by and brought them their orders as they sat, sipped and observed. Mahogany and Melanie hadn't been to DC since their childhood they had to admit it felt damn good with all the love their new faces were getting. They were now 40 years old but didn't look a day over 20 and were hired hit women. Their first kill was their mother, Michelle, when they were 15 years old and since then they been on their own murdering for hire.

 Just as Destiny was about to walk over and introduce herself she saw her sister, Valerie, walk in and sit with the twins. They talked for about twenty minutes before Valerie pulled out an envelope that looked to be pretty thick and handed to Mahogany. She sat silently observing the three, wondering what they could be talking about until they all left. She made a mental note to go back before the night was over but missed them.

Chapter 7

Weeks had gone by and it was finally the day Destiny had marked to visit her brother, Supreme. She hadn't gotten a reply from the last letter she sent him and hoped that things went well today. Just as she was getting dressed there was a hard knock on the door. She wasn't expecting any company and VJ had a key which made her side eye the front door. "Who could this be?" she asked herself as she stood on her tip toes to look out of the peephole but when she looked it was as if someone was covering it she snatched it open and there stood her big brother Supreme.

"Oh my god 'Preme!!" she shouted as she jumped up and wrapped her arms around his neck.

Usually Destiny hated surprises, but this was one she welcomed. She cried tears of joy.

"Hey baby sis. How are you?" Supreme smiled as he hugged his little sister tight. When he got her letter, he didn't bother writing back but instead chose to surprise her in person.

"I was just getting dressed to come see you." Destiny said as Supreme placed her back on her feet.

"Well I'm here to see you what's up?" Supreme smiled as he took a seat on the sofa.

"Well let me whip you up some food. I know you hungry. Then I'll get into everything else." Destiny said as she

An Uneasy Truth 2

walked into the kitchen to cook. After Destiny was done cooking they ate while getting into deep conversation regarding the incident with their sister Valerie. Supreme vowed to get to the bottom of things ensuring Destiny all would be well.

"I gotta make a few runs around the city." I'll swing through later to chill with you and my nephew, he's coming back, tonight right?" Supreme stood and stretched that meal his little sister whipped up had him getting the itis.

"Yeah he should. He's got friends he actually likes to be around, so I've been letting him experience that." Destiny laughed she noticed VJ and Lem had been getting very close lately and thought it was adorable seeing Lem is Isis only son and VJ an only child they both yearned for some brotherly love.

"Ok, let me put my cell number in your phone." Supreme said reaching for Destiny's cellphone before walking toward the front door.

"Aight 'Preme I love you be safe. And call me." Destiny said as she hugged her big brother before he walked out the door. This made Destiny's day her brother was free, and things were looking up already.

Supreme watched as a royal blue Chevy Tahoe pulled up in front of him and the passenger window rolled down.

"What's good playboy." Chinc said greeting his cousin.

"This good freedom air my nigga. Where we headed?" Supreme smiled as he climbed inside.

"Straight to the mall my nigga." Chinc asked prepared to make sure his cousin was good, he was finally home, and it was time he lived like the king he was. They hit the mall and grabbed everything Supreme needed then cruised to the bar where Supreme met with one of his good homies who owned the bar and hired him to work at the bar a few nights a week, Supreme was grateful. He and Chinc celebrated his homecoming as well as his new gig for a few hours over drinks as they joked and socialized.

Chinc offered to treat Supreme to Club Spread however he declined. He chose to go cool it with his sister and nephew instead so Chinc dropped him off and went on his way.

Chapter 8
Club Spread

"What the fuck you mean we not gonna be together Leo?"

Kasey screamed at Leo, she was tired of being good enough to fuck but never good enough to fuck with.

"Look you already knew what it was. Whatever we had is done." Leo said as he attempted to walk pass Kasey. He and Kasey had been sleeping together for months though Leo was in a steady relationship with his long time girlfriend Truth. He managed to keep sexing up Kasey knowing it was bad for business because she was a dancer at Club Spread and now she was pregnant again this being her second pregnancy by Leo, He didn't want a child or anything else from Kasey but sex on demand he had no intentions on leaving Truth for anybody.

Kasey couldn't take it anymore. This would be the second pregnancy he was asking her to have and on top of that he dismissed her as if she was nothing. Her last pregnancy was stomped out of her by some girls trying to rob her. She flew into a rage, punching Leo dead in the face and following up raining blows on him as he covered his head and attempted to get away from her. She was on him every step he took, though. After trying to peel her off Leo the bouncers tossed her out the club. She then began busting out the windows of his car. She was determined to make him pay by all means before she left the premises. Just as she was about to get in her car she saw a baby diaper laying in the parking lot and smeared the shitty diaper all over his car.

"Oh, this not over nigga I'mma go see this bitch of yours next…" Kasey said to herself as she cruised passed the police cars the sped in the direction of the club.

Leo looked on at the damage Kasey left behind and shook his head this was all his fault Ali told him that fucking with her was a bad look and he persuade anyway. He pulled out his cellphone and called his mother the only woman in the world he loved more than anything and her opinion he trusted.

"Hello." Pam answered on the third ring.

"Ma, you not even gonna believe this shit. Check out the shit I just sent you." Leo said referring to the pictures of his car he had sent just before making the call.

"What the fuck?!? And let me guess your hard-headed ass kept fucking with that stripper bitch, right?" Pam asked with sass dripping from her words. She'd warned her son on numerous occasions about fucking around on his woman and the consequences it would bring.

"That's not the point, I need you to go get Truth from the airport for me please." Leo said with a bit of aggravation.

"Sure son." Pam said before hanging up on Leo and calling Truth to confirm where she needs to be picked up from.

Chapter 9
Isis

*I*sis pulled up to P.G college parked and walked in to the administrator's office. She finally felt like she could take on school again. She signed her paperwork and headed to the fashion department she needed to catch Professor Stewart before he left for the day.

"Oh, great Professor Stewart I caught you." Isis said out of breath with a grin.

"Ohhh well welcome back Ms. Monroe. How may I help you?" Professor Stewart asked happy to see Isis, a lot of other business professionals had been asking about her work.

"I'm stopping by to gather any notes or assignments I may have missed or should be caught up on." Isis said

"Oh yes, and by the way young lady your portfolio has been pretty popular amongst my colleagues." He said as he passed her a packet of work and notes.

"Oh, thank you so much, Really? That's great to know thank you." Isis said beaming

An Uneasy Truth 2

"As a matter of fact, you are one of the most talented young ladies in my class that is why I recommended you for this Paris fashion week experience." He said taking a seat in his chair waiting for Isis reaction.

"OH MY GOD! PARIS?!" Isis was in pure shock standing there with her mouth partially open.

"Look over this information and let me know if you would like to participate have a two week to get back to me we leave in a month in a half considering passports and booking arrangements. Just email me all my information is also on this paper as well." Professor Stewart said handing her the sheet of paper with all the trip information on it. He was pleased with his decision to choose her for this trip she was very talented in his eyes.

"Oh, wow Professor, I will take all this in and get back with you. Thank you." Isis said before leaving the college and heading to her car. She took a picture of the paper and sent it to Mel, Shell and Nadine then started her car and pulled off she felt awesome inside who does shit like this happen to. "Me that's who." she thought to herself as she drove home in her thoughts.

As she parked in front of her building her cellphone buzzed indicating she had a text message.

Mommy: I need to talk to you.

Isis: When?

Mommy: ASAP

Isis: I'll be over in an hour.

She needed to go inside and make sure the kids were fed and together for bed before. She headed over to Nadine's she had no idea what it could be she need to talk to her about asap, but she was sure about to find out.

Nadine hung up with Loco after discussing the results of the paternity test they had done a few weeks prior with a sample Isis' hair and Loco's DNA and thought about if what she was about to tell Isis was even a good idea, but Loco was right the truth must be told. A little over an hour went by when Isis came walking through the front door.

"Hey mommy, what's up? You okay?" Isis asked as she took a seat next to her mother who was slowly sipping on a wine cooler as Sam Cooke play low on the stereo system.

"I love you and you need to know every decision I've ever made I made because I thought it was best for all my children." Nadine began as tear threatened to fall from her eyes, when she looked into Isis' face she could see the perfect combination of herself and Loco.

"Mommy what are you talking about?" Isis asked with a confused look on her face, she didn't know where this was going but decided to remove the wine cooler from Nadine's hand and sit it on the table. "Maybe it's this shit." She thought to herself.

"Markel is not your father. Loco is your father." Nadine didn't waste any more time, her daughter was 29 years old and had been living a lie. Isis sat processing what Nadine had just told her.

"Mommy damn. That's some shit to process at 30." Isis said as she picked up Nadine's wine cooler and tossed it back finishing it off.

"Why now mommy? Is he any of our father?" Isis asked looking her mother in her eyes she remembered all too well how Markel just abandoned them.

"Because it's time you know besides Loco thinks its time you should know. Markel is Mel and Shells father but not yours, You also have two older sisters and…" Nadine explained but Isis cut her off.

An Uneasy Truth 2

"That's enough mommy. Go to bed I can't deal right now. My son just murdered his father. Shell is sabotaging Markel. Now, this man I have been looking up to a big part of my life, you are telling me is actually my biological father not the man who I actually thought is my father who abandoned us, not to mention I just got offered the biggest opportunity in the fashion industry on the other side of the world. I need to go this is a lot to process. Love you mommy." Isis said before walking out of the front door locking it with her key behind her.

Nadine felt a sense of relief as she made her way to her room, feeling a little buzz from the wine coolers she'd drank. She changed her clothes and climbed into bed. She lay there thinking of the reason for her doing the things she did back then until she drifted off to sleep.

Chapter 10

Loco sat at the trap counting money at the kitchen table when Black walked in looking disturbed.

"What's good young blood?" Loco asked as Black took a seat across from him at the table.

"I should've head shot that nigga. I put his ass down and he come back and still get my girl unc." Black said as he clasps his hands together and placed them under his chin. Loco sat for a second as Blacks words floated around his brain. He had an idea what he was speaking of but decided to pick Blacks brain instead.

"Elaborate young blood. You ranting." Loco chuckled.

"Dat nigga Troy. I heard somebody took care of Vee bitchass. But oh, he was next." Black explained.

"Oh yea? Where you hear that?" Smurf interjected as he walked into the kitchen.

"What's up Unc. Apparently, the cleaner bitch we had on the team was Vee other baby mother Vanessa, Vicky, Val something like that well she was sent to the removal and said a kid had the smoking gun but any who she seen it was dat nigga and disappeared from the scene." Black broke it down. Word travels fast in the streets.

"Fuuuck that's why this bitch been Missing in action and hit me about a hitman?" Smurf said before quickly putting things together and making a call on his cellphone.

"Word is she taking that shit hard." Black continued.

"Fuck man.!" Smurf said as he slammed his fist on the table.

"What's up Smurf?" Loco asked feeling uneasy.

"Find the Twins. That's who info I gave her." Smurf said in a somber tone shaking his head.

"Wait what's going on?" Black asked sensing something wasn't right, he had most of the details but not all and Loco left it that way.

"Ay young blood we gon' holla at you later." Loco said dismissing Black. Black respected both Loco and Smurf so he stood and dapped them both up and left.

They looked at each other knowing things could get really ugly.

Destiny

"Aunt Destiny is it ok for me to go with Jahmier and Lem with their uncle to the movies?" VJ asked innocently in hopes that Destiny would say yes.

He hadn't been back home with Valerie and didn't think twice about it. He enjoyed just being a kid with other kids and he felt a sense of closeness to Lem and Jahmier now Sky she was always side eyeing him like she was trying to figure him out and where he came from.

"Your room clean and did you finish your project?" Destiny asked in a motherly tone.

"Yes." He said as he reached for his vibrating cellphone. It was Lem asking him if he could go with them because they were leaving out soon.

"Yeah I guess so and you better behave." Destiny said as she watched him take off down the hall to get ready. Thirty minutes later Mel, Lem and Jamier tapped on Destiny's door.

"Oh, Heyy guys." Destiny said as she hugged Lem and Jahmier then stepped aside to allow the three in.

"Damn. I'm sorry. How you doing I'm Destiny." Destiny stammered. She was intrigued by Mel he was chocolate, about 6-foot 2 solid build with long locs and handsome. "Shit Isis is pretty but her brother is fine as hell." She thought to herself as her eyes traced him from head to toe.

"Hey how you doing miss lady. Is VJ ready?" Mel blushed a little. She was sexy, but he didn't geek if they crossed paths again it would be what it would be. He made a mental note to ask Isis about her though.

"Oh I'm sorry. Yeah he's ready." She said before walking away to go get him from the room.

"Hey little man Lem and the gang are here to get you, are you ready?" Destiny said peeping her head in the bedroom.

"Yup." VJ said as he tossed his controller on the bed and walked into the living room and out the door.

"Well see you later little boy!" Destiny yelled down the hall behind him as he and Lem races down the hall.

An Uneasy Truth 2

"All of them are going to Isis house afterward, you will be able to get him from there? If not, I can bring him back.

"You can bring him back if you don't mind." Destiny said with a grin.

Mel nodded and left to catch up with the boys, when he got in the car he texted Isis telling her to send him Destiny's number in case of any emergency she did, and he locked it in. She was cute he wasn't geeking but if she biting he was all for it. He took the boys out to the movies and to dinner at Applebee's everyone was enjoying themselves. Once they arrived at Isis apartment the boys all gathered in Lem's room to play video games and talk about the movie.

"Who are your parents? How come you only come over with your aunt?" Sky asked leaning in Lem's doorway looking VJ dead in the eyes.

"Why you always grill him when he come over Sky?" Lem asked with a chuckle. He didn't understand Sky's problem. She walked up on Lem never breaking their eye contact.

"Because he just fell out of nowhere and he look like daddy. That's not odd to you?" Sky replied low through clenched teeth so that only Lem could hear her. Lem glanced at VJ taking in what Sky had just said after she walked out of his room. He knew his little sister was like a blood hound when she felt like she was on to something and didn't stop until the truth was told.

Isis sat on the couch flipping through channels when Sky came a sat down next to her.

"What you watching mommy? Sky asked plopping down on the couch laying her head across Isis' lap.

"Don't seem like its much on to watch baby. You okay?" Isis asked stroking Sky's cheek.

Sky explained what was bothering her including VJ looking like Vee and nobody notices it. Isis sat pondering Sky's words and she was right he did favor Vee. Isis decided to put it to the back of her mind the world was small but how small was it. As she sat listening to Sky her cellphone rang.

"Hey cuz." Isis said happily seeing it was her cousin Charli, she hadn't spoken to her in over a year she was glad to hear from her.

"Hey baby, how are you? I spoke to Shell she filled me in already. Are the kids ok?" Charli shot off questions.

"Yes, we are all good. How are you?" Isis replied she made a mental note to talk to Shell, she understood they were all close at some point and family, but she didn't want the entire family knowing Lem killed his father.

"Things are what they are." Charli said in a disappointed tone.

"You still with Ali? He just opened that new club not too long, ago right?" Isis asked

"Yeah we still sticking it out. Shit gets old you know? Mu'fuckas get tired of being emotionally abused." Charli said honestly.

"Yeah I feel you. How's Truth?"

"Oh, she is really good, she just got offered to model for Jon Marc in Paris." Charli said instantly pepping up she was proud of her little cousin.

"Well that makes two of us. My teacher nominated me to go to assist a few local designers who are showcasing during Paris fashion week." Isis said with excitement, knowing her cousin was going to Paris eased her mind a bit at least she wouldn't be going alone.

An Uneasy Truth 2

"Oh my god! That is great cuz. I'm going to text Truth your number now so y'all can chat once we get off the phone. I'm so proud of y'all." Charli said sincerely.

"Thanks cuz, I appreciate that." Isis said now smiling it felt good to hear that.

"Mommy you going to Paris?" Sky said jumping up off Isis' lap. She had been laying there just listening to the speakerphone conversation which is why Isis didn't go into full detail about the chain of events.

"Yes baby girl." Isis smiled feeling a since of pride in herself.

"Oh, cuz let me give you a call back I need to email my teacher." Isis said before ending her call, and opening her Gmail app to email Professor Stewart.

"What do VJ stand for anyway?" Jahmier asked looking at VJ he was now seeing what Sky was saying when she said he looked like a bad memory.

"Vaughn Junior." VJ said nonchalantly before turning his attention back to the game.

"WHAT?!" Lem asked instantly pausing the game.

"Oooh shit." Jahmier said under his breath.

"Vaughn Junior. What? Why you pause the game?" VJ was confused he didn't know what he said that had just upset Lem, but he could see the fire in his eyes. Jahmier slid back on the bed placing his back on the wall as he looked on at what would transpire.

"What's your dads name?" Lem asked sitting his controller on the floor in front of him turning to completely face VJ. VJ now felt a little uneasy he too sat his controller down as well.

"My dad's name is Vee." He replied. He didn't know why Lem was asking who he was or why it mattered but he didn't feel the need to hide the fact.

"OH MY GOD!" Jahmier shouted as Isis walked in the room.

"Hey VJ, you ready to go yet?" she asked unaware of the conversation that was taking place upon her entry.

"So that makes you my brother?" Lem asked as he sat confused.

"Huh?" VJ said with his face filled with confusion, he didn't understand because how could he have a brother when his mother told him he was the only child when he use to ask about brothers and sisters. Isis stood eyes wide when she heard what Lem said.

"What are y'all talking about?" Isis said as she looked from Lem to VJ then over to Jahmier with one hand on her hip.

"Mommy he just said his dad is my dad. How is that if he not your child?" Lem asked seriously he didn't understand.

"Umm Ummm he what?" Isis said with a nervous chuckle, unable to process what Lem said the first time.

"Auntie he just said his dads name is Vee." Jahmier said timidly. Isis didn't know what to say considering this too was shocking news to her.

"You know guys people have the exact same name all the time this could just be a coincidence." Isis said with a grin.

"I told Y'all he looked like our daddy." Sky said with her arms folded over her chest.

"Take your little self in the living room please." Isis said with a little irritation. Sky sucked her teeth and went back into the living room.

An Uneasy Truth 2

"Do y'all know my dad or something?" VJ asked sensing the tension in the room grow thick.

"Know him? That's my father." Lem said now really looking at VJ seeing him as a younger looking Vee, their father.

"Hold up y'all!" Isis began but was cut off by Lem.

"Nahh mama it's no coincidence. This is my brother." Lem said staring VJ in the eyes.

Isis looked on between the two and didn't know what to say or do.

"Mama uncle Mel on your cellphone." Sky said handing Isis her cellphone.

"Hello." Isis said walking back into the living room out of earshot of the kids.

"Hey sis. You alright you sound shook." Mel inquired.

"We were having a great time until we learned Vee is VJ's father." Isis replied in a hushed tone.

"What? How you figure?" Mel asked in confusion.

"Right. Well I'm not 100% on how the information came about I just know I walked in the room to see if VJ was ready like you texted asking me to do and walked in on VJ telling Jahmier and Lem his father's name is Vee." Isis said as she took a seat on the couch and rubbed her hands through her hair.

"I'm on my way to Destiny's I'mma just bring her over there so things can be explained or whatever." Mel said as he climbed in his car and headed to Destiny's apartment. He called Destiny once he was outside and they headed over to Isis' apartment. On the way there, Mel told Destiny the current situation as she listened she tried to wrap her head around how this was possible.

Knock knock... Mel knocked on the door

"Heyyy..." Isis said as she opened the door and let them both in.

"Hey. Isis, I honestly don't know how this is possible." Destiny explained as she took a seat on the couch next to VJ.

"Well auntie this is my dad. It's real." VJ said sounding a bit agitated as he lifted a picture from the photo album Isis had brought out of her room trying to clear things up. All his life he'd wanted a sibling and always being told he didn't have one, yet he had two. He didn't know whether to be angry with Vee or Valerie.

I'm calling Valerie." Destiny said as she pulled out her cellphone. VJ stopped her.

"Nahh auntie no need." VJ said in a down tone. He felt like he'd been shorted.

"Ayy VJ Lem wants you in the room." Jahmier said before running back down the hall.

"Say bye and come on VJ." Destiny said feeling overwhelmed.

"What's up Lem?" VJ said with a nod as he stuck his hands in his pocket.

"You are my brother, so you need to know who your father is before you go. He's an evil, angry, woman beater and he's dead." Lem said with no remorse.

"What? How could you say something like that my daddy ain't never been none of those things?" VJ said defensively.

An Uneasy Truth 2

"Oh, but he is VJ, we don't know what he used to do with you and your mama but he beat ours even almost killed her once. So that nigga had to go." Sky said sassily as she sat down on Lem's bed and crossed her arms.

"That's not true. And how you know he dead?" Lem said with his fist balled up in his pockets.

"'Cause I killed him." Lem said, through clinched teeth as he stepped into VJ's face.

"What?!" VJ said through squinted eyes, before he knew it he swung on Lem, Lem dodged the blow and hit VJ in the side with a body blow to each side. Mel could hear tussling as he walked passed the bedroom from the bathroom in the hall and opened the door the VJ and Lem squaring up like grown men he stopped them immediately and sat them down.

"Check this out y'all brothers blood is thicker than anything. Y'all supposed to stick together not fight each other. Yes, both of y'all found out this information in a wild way but the fact of the matter is y'all are brothers." Mel said.

"But Mel he killed our father." VJ said through tears.

"I would do it again if I had to protect my family again." Lem said swelling his chest up.

"Wait what?! First of all, Lem deflate yourself you ain't murk nobody and secondly VJ truth be told and as bad as it may hurt to know he had that coming. And I know you don't understand because he was good to you and your mom, but they don't know the side of the guy you call your father." Mel explained as he pulled VJ in and hugged him tight. He knew how it felt to discover your father ain't the hero you thought he was.

"Uncle Mel, what you mean I pulled the trigger three times." Lem said as he held his imaginary pistol and shot into the air.

"Nephew. Trust your uncle you didn't. Now let that shit go hug it out." Mel told them refusing to let them know it was he who sent that head shot and killed Vee instantly.

"Uncle Mel can you tell Auntie I think I'mma stay, I wanna get to know my brother and sister." VJ said after he and Lem released their embrace.

"What about me?" Jahmier asked innocently.

"You too cousin I ain't forget about you." VJ said. All three bursts into laughter and hugged.

"No problem nephew. And Sky quit all that dat Nancy Drew shit out man ok? " Mel said after hugging Sky.

"Nancy who?" Sky questioned she had no clue who he was talking about.

"Never mind." He laughed as hugged Jahmier before leaving the room. Mel walked out into the living room and let Destiny and Isis know what had transpired and how he defused the situation and that they all wanted to get to know each other more tonight, Destiny and Isis were fine with that. They said their goodbyes then Mel and Destiny left. Mel and Destiny rode around for a while getting to know one another.

The next night Destiny thought it would be best to take VJ home to Valerie, he had a lot of questions that only she could answer being his mother. Then she texted Isis to see if she was down to go out to Club Spread it was open mic night and from everything that Isis had hanging on her she thought a good outing was just what she needed. Isis was with an outing since all the kids were at Shell's and Troy was working out of town and she didn't have any other plans.

LOCO

An Uneasy Truth 2

After learning that Valerie had paid Melanie and Mahogany to kill Isis he made several failed attempts to reach them. After contacting Leo, he found out that Club Spread was one of their favorite spots to hit up mainly because that's where Leo usually was and since they were able to get out of Cali wherever he was they weren't too far away.

Loco walked into Club spread and took a seat near the back where he could see everything from all angles. He didn't really care for clubs but understood why Leo got involved in the business as he looked around at all the half-dressed beautiful curvy women of all shapes and sizes and shades.

"Its 'bout to be poppin'." Destiny said bouncing in her seat to Fat Trel's latest hit as it blared through Isis' speakers.

"It better be." Isis teased as she parked her car not far from the entrance. They stepped out the car and all eyes were on them as they made their way to the door. Destiny had become popular in the short time she had been working there and the bouncers loved her, so they allowed them in with no hesitation.

They say at a table off to the side of the stage Loco watched as they entered, had a seat and ordered drinks but suddenly it was as if time started moving slow when Melanie and Mahogany walked in, neither of them saw him but he watched as they noticed Isis and Destiny.

"Sis that's a two for one 3 o'clock." Melanie whispered to Mahogany nodding in Isis and Destiny's direction. Mahogany nodded in agreement.

"Cousin Lo?" Leo asked as he walked passed the table and noticed Loco tucked in the corner.

"Leo. What's good youngsta?" Loco said as they embraced in a man hug.

"I'm good I'm good, you know Mel and Ma-ma in, here right?" Leo replied

"I'm watching. Don't even tell them I'm here." Loco said as he took a sip of his Hennessy and coke.

"No problem and whatever you drinking it's on me." Leo said before dapping up Loco and stepping off to attend to business.

Loco waited until the crowd started to get thick before maneuvering through the crowd in Melanie and Mahogany's direction, he crept up on them silently just as he got closer Mahogany spun around quickly and quietly pointing her pistol on Loco.

"Hey daddy." She smiled before tucking her weapon and jumping off her seat to hug her father. Melanie followed suit, they were happy to see their father.

"How my girls doin'?" Loco asked stepping back to look at the two.

"We good daddy." Melanie replied as she pulled up a chair for him. Loco took a seat between the two he noticed their attention on Isis and Destiny.

"I been trying to get in contact with y'all for weeks." Loco said looking between the two.

"We been on the job." Mahogany said never taking her eyes off Isis who was now partying to one of the local artist on stage.

"That's your mark?" Loco asked nodding toward Isis' direction.

"Yes." Mahogany said slowly turning her head toward Loco and staring him straight in the eye.

An Uneasy Truth 2

"That's your sister. You can't touch her." Loco said as he began reminding them of the day they went to D.C with him to Nadine's house.

"Oh, Shit that's Isis? OH MY GOD." Melanie said as she covered her mouth in shock. Their number one rule when taking a hit is no names but had this gone through they would've murdered their little sister, Mahogany felt fucked up this was one time doing what she loved to do would've ruined her life.

"Oh, so you already know what that mean?" Melanie said as she looked into Mahogany's eyes it was as if they were communicating through their minds because seconds later they each kissed Loco on the cheek and promised to call him the next day before they left the club.

Loco was relieved now he tossed back the remainder of his drink and found Leo to let him know he was leaving. As he rode home he thought about how things could've went all wrong for his family tonight and how blessed he was to had been in the right place at the right time. When he reached Nadine's apartment he showered and cuddle up under her. "Yeah I'm blessed." He thought to himself before drifting off to sleep.

Isis woke up with the worst hangover she had been hanging out with Destiny the past few weeks and now she was days away from the Paris trip. She peeled herself off the sheets and made it to the shower the hot water gave her just enough energy to wash and make some bacon on her George Foreman grill and get right back in the bed.

"Mama you want me to help you pack?" Sky said as she bust through Isis bedroom door with a big smile on her face. "Does this kid read my mind or something?" Isis thought to herself as she chuckled and threw the comforter over her head.

"Yes, baby girl, just not right now." Isis said regretfully knowing she had to eventually get up. Sky snatched the comforter back and kissed her forehead.

"I'll be back then , be up mommy." Sky said as she took off out the room and down the hall. Isis saw that she had a few missed texts, so she checked them as she swung her legs over the side of the bed, there was a text from Nadine saying Sunday dinner was at her house and not optional. "Fuck what day is it?" Isis said aloud as she swiped to the calendar on her phone. Just as she laid her phone on the bed and walk away to get herself together for the day her cellphone began ringing she walked back over to pick it up and to her surprise it was Black.

"Hey, Black, what's up?" she answered happy to hear from him it had been awhile since she heard from him he was Vee's right hand man but still a dear friend.

"Isis, I need to talk to you." He said sounding a little off.

"Okay I'll be around Benning Court in a few hours, can we meet up then?" she replied

"Oh okay, call me when you get around here and Isis please don't forget." Black said before hanging up.

Isis looked at the screen a little confused because Black didn't sound like himself she made a mental note to make sure she called him as soon as she got around the way. In the meantime, she needed to shake this hangover all the way off. A few hours later Isis, Lem and Sky were dressed and headed to Nadine's apartment, Isis figured if she got there early she would be able to take a short nap before dinner. However, Nadine had a surprise in store it was time she let all the cats out the bag.

Nadine had prepared a beautiful dinner, Roast beef with carrots and potatoes, peppers and onions, Fresh collard greens, fried chicken, baked macaroni and cheese, steamed broccoli, white rice, cornbread and biscuits. She stood back to look at the spread she had really out done herself, but it was worth it she loved her family.

Loco walked up behind her and places gently kisses on the back of her neck causing her to heat up she almost got lost in the moment when there was a rhythmic knock at the door. "Damn." Loco whispered

"Oh, that's desert." Nadine said with a wink as she walked away to get the door. Loco smiled and anticipated desert as he walked to the bathroom to finish putting his clothes on. He and Nadine had been inseparable since the night Vee took her hostage.

"Hey Hey now." Pam said as she walked through the door with joy. She hugged Nadine for a long time she was happy to see her best friend once again.

"Things are about to come full circle now fo'sho." Pam said with giggled.

"You damn right. Hey cuz." Loco said with a smile as he and Pam embraced in a long hug.

"Heyy mommy." Mel, Shell and Jahmier walked in the door.

"Heyy babies." Nadine said as she hugged them each.

"Grandmaaaa!" Sky yelled as she bolted through the door and wrapped herself around Nadine who was sitting on the couch.

"Sky baby, you gonna kill your poor grandmother. Hey mommy" Isis said shaking her head laughing as she leaned down to where Nadine was sitting and kissed her on the cheek. She hadn't seen Nadine since she gave her that unexpected information. "Guess I'm not the only one with the bright idea to come early." Isis thought to herself seeing her opportunity to lay down go out the window.

"Dang girl let me hug my grandma." Lem said snatching Sky off Nadine's lap. Everyone started to laugh.

"I got enough love for you both. Now cut it out." Nadine said as she pulled Lem beside her hugging him. After a few minutes of everyone talking there was a knock at the door. In walked Smurf and Leo.

"Hey hey now." Smurf said with a smile as he and Leo greeted everyone, and Pam introduced him to his cousins.

"Mama I can eat right?" Mel said as he walked up to the table looking at all the delicious food Nadine prepared.

"Not yet. We're waiting on a few more guest." Nadine said with a smile she was feeling pretty good about this gathering. Just as she stood up there was another knock at the door, she opened it and there stood her nieces Charli and Truth she smiled.

"Auntie!!" they both screamed in unison as three hugged.

"Look at you two. Come on in your cousins are here already." Nadine said as she stepped aside to allow them in. Just as she was closing the door she could hear two female voices bickering back and forth.

"Did you write the address, down right?" Mahogany asked Melanie as she snatched the paper out of her hand that had Nadine's address written on it.

"Don't do it. Of course, I did." Melanie replied with attitude.

"You two looking for me?" Nadine said with a smile and on hand on her hip as she stood at the top of the stairs.

An Uneasy Truth 2

"Aww Nadineee!" they shouted as they hurried and got to the top of the stairs to hug her. They were so happy to see her well and looking just as young as the day they met her. Ever since she spent that week in Cali they loved her and secretly wished she was their mom instead of the demon they were birthed to however they sent her where she deserved to be hell.

Nadine wrapped them with as much love as she could muster she remembered how she felt knowing they would be headed back to Michelle and wished she could've done more. "No better time than the present." Nadine thought to herself as she gave them each a motherly kiss on the cheek and they all walked inside.

"Truth what you doing here?" Leo asked confused as he walked from the bathroom.

"Isis is my cousin. What are you doing here?" Truth replied with a puzzled look on her face.

"Wait! WHAT! She's my cousin too." Leo said as he looked toward Nadine then his mom waiting for one of them to chime in because things are looking like he had been in a relationship with his cousin for over 5 years. He was starting to feel physically sick at the thought.

"Aww shit. This sounds like some Jerry springer messiness." Shell said as she sipped her soda and sat back on the couch as if this was a television episode.

"Shut up Shell." Mel said laughing as he tossed a small throw pillow at her.

"Ok I see where this is going." Nadine said in laughter "Leo you are not blood related to Truth. Her father is my brother who married her mom when she was two months old. So, there is no blood relation.

"Thank Gawwd!" Sky said as she fakes fainting in the middle of the floor causing everyone to burst into laughter.

"Get your daughter!" Jahmier said to Isis in laughter.

"Who are these beautiful ladies?" Mel asked referring to the twins.

"These are Isis older sisters, Mahogany and Melanie." Nadine introduced them.

"Wait what? Why just Isis sisters?" Shell asked looking confused, Isis hadn't told her the conversation she and Nadine had about Markel not being her father.

"Well Shell Markel isn't my father he's you and Mel's dad, Loco is my father." Isis explained as she looked over at Loco who smiled warmly.

"Well damn." Shell said in a shocked tone.

"This is definitely a Jerry Springer night auntie." Sky said as she glanced around the room at all the fresh faces.

"Can we eat now? Or we waiting on Jesus next?" Mel said in a joking tone.

"Yes boy." Nadine said as she got up to pray over the food and fix the children's plates. They all ate and conversed for hours. The twins even explained to Isis how they were hired to kill her and how they were happy Loco stopped them. Isis looked over at Loco who was in conversation with Smurf, Leo, and Mel and silently thanked god he was her father he may not have spent all her life with her, but he was definitely with her all her life.

After everyone had eaten, chatted and now had the itis it was time to wrap things up they all exchanged information and promised to keep in contact. Truth and Isis even made plans to fly to Paris together in the next few days.

Knock knock

An Uneasy Truth 2

"You expecting somebody?" Shell turned from the table where she was making her to-go plate to ask Nadine.

"No." Nadine said nonchalantly.

"I'll get it." Loco said as he walked to answer the door.

"The fuck is you doing here?" Loco asked with his now happy expression balled into a mug.

"Ain't you supposed to be in jail or something nigga? Get the fuck out my way." Markel said as he attempted to storm passed Loco.

CLICK "Oh no sir this ain't what you want." Mahogany said in a menacing tone as she pressed the barrel of her pistol between Markel's eyes. Loco definitely didn't expect that but welcomed it.

"SHELL GET THE FUCK OUT HERE!" Markel shouted as he stood at the door frozen in place with the cold barrel of a chrome 45 pressed against his head.

"What the fuck do you want?" Shell asked as she came flying out the front door. She was over Markel she felt like she ain't do shit to him that he ain't been doing all her life, fucking 'em over.

"I know it was you. It was you that tried to ruin everything I've built." Markel yelled with spit foaming at the corner of his mouth. He was angry and wanted payback.

"What you built? Fuck what you built it never involved us so fuck it and fuck you, I ain't got time to argue." Shell said before quickly cocking back her fist and hitting Markel with so much force he fell backward down the stairs breaking his neck. No one saw the blow coming she moved so fast, Mahogany still had her pistol in the same position it was against his head when he tumbled down the stairs.

"Uncle Smurf take out the trash. Come on Jahmier." Shell said as she stepped over her father's body on her way down the stairs. Smurf dialed up the cleaners after checking his pulse and did as his niece asked had the trash disposed of as Everyone got their food and went their separate ways. That put a damper on the night, but Nadine made sure to keep her word and give Loco that desert.

Chapter 11
***Isis (Paris) Present**

I never thought that I would be where I am today. What started out as a dream has manifested into reality and to put the icing on the cake my cousin too is living her dreams walking in a few fashion shows. As we sat in the airport, surrounding by noise and chattering people, I am nervous about this new journey. I hope that Paris is all that I read about in magazines. My stomach tightened at the idea of being on an airplane for 8 hours but it will all be worth it in the end. All of the blood, sweat, and tears I have put into my craft will finally pay off. Truth squeezed my hand I guess she could sense my nervousness.

"Now boarding gate C5." The announcers voice rang out.

We looked up and then gathered our carry on items. Looking over my shoulder, I thought about all I was leaving behind for a while. The plane was enormous and I had first class seats. I put my bag into the overhead and sat comfortably in my seat, unfortunately Truth and I aren't able to sit together since the travel agent could get us on the same flight and same hotel we sacrificed not being able to sit together. As our flight was about to take off, a gentleman sat next to me. He was tall and slender with a low cut. He smiled politely and then, put his headphones in. Then, the flight attended stood at the end of the seats and leaned down to say something.

"Can I offer you anything? Champagne, wine? Or food?"

"Sure," I said nervously. "I will have a glass of champagne and a burger."

"Sure." She smiled and quickly walked away.

"I can get use to this." I mumbled under my breath.

At first I was so restless, I couldn't get comfortable but then, I fell asleep. There was really nothing else to do on the long flight to paradise. When the guy next to me woke up, he decided he wanted to start a conversation.

"Where are you from?"

"DC." I answered with a slight smile.

"Oh," He nodded, "me too. I'm headed to Paris's Fashion Week."

I laughed and said, "Me, too. You don't strike me as a fashion type of guy."

"You mean, I'm not gay."

I looked away. "Uh..."

"I'm DaCool MicL, owner and designer of Imajean Collection."

I was a little embarrassed. His brand was the latest fashion wave of the tri-state area but more importantly of the Hip-Hop culture. I have seen many artist and reality television stars wearing his clothing. I sat there next to him, judging him.

"I'm sorry."

"No, it's okay. I get that reaction a lot. It says you know much about the culture of creativity." He brushed it off. "Do you have a line?"

I took a sip of my champagne, "Uh, no. I'm new to all of this." I looked around.

"Oh, don't be modest. I am sure there are many talents up your sleeves."

I smiled. I wasn't sure if he was flirting but I liked the sound of his voice. He was different than all of the other men in DC. I was use to gangsters; shooters and cheaters. MicL struck me as a educated hippy. I would bet that he smoked a whole lot of weed.

An Uneasy Truth 2

When the plane finally landed, there was someone in the lobby of the airport waiting for me with a sign with my name on it. I said good bye to MicL and followed the driver out to the town car that awaited. I sent Truth a text letting her know I was in route to the hotel and that I would see her when she got there. There was a bottle of wine and a tray of dark chocolate covered strawberries. I didn't touch it though. I spent the entire ride staring out of the window. There were some tall people in Paris. All of them were different shades of unique. I smiled with appreciation for the opportunity to be apart of this epic experience.

The car arrived at my hotel and the driver came to let me out.

You'll be able to exchange your currency inside." He told me, carrying my bags to the door. "Here is my card, call me whenever you're wanting to go out."

"Thank you," I nodded pulling a ten dollar bill out of my purse. I handed it to him.

"My darling, this is much too much. I will wait until you've exchanged your currency." He smiled and walked away.

I stepped into the hotel, taken aback by its beauty. The ceilings were tall and hollow, bearing breathtaking art of angels and water. I looked around, almost with tears in my eyes. I stood there for several moments with my hands on my chest.

"Hello, may I help you?" a woman asked.

I turned to her and placed my purse on the counter. "Yes, I have a reservation." I told her pulling out the fax with all of my information.

"Uh, yes." She typed something on the computer. Then, she handed me a key. "Room 1122. On the elevator up to the 11th floor and to your left." She instructed and smiled.

"Thank you."

"Someone will be bringing your bags up shortly." She waved.

"Thanks." I went to press the button for the elevator.

"Let me get that for you." I heard a familiar baritone.

"What are the odds?" I asked, smiling at him.

"You tell me, Ms. Isis." MicL took my bag.

We stepped on the elevator and I pressed the eleventh floor. He didn't press any number. "Please, don't tell me you're on the eleventh floor, too." I shook my head. "Either that or you're stalking me," I laughed half-jokingly.

"What would make you think so terribly of me?" he frowned.

"You really don't sound like you're from DC." I chuckled as the elevator doors opened. "Are you sure you're not just putting on to get with me?"

"That's ridiculous." He handed me the bag. "I think you're a lovely young lady but you're reaching."

I frowned. "Good bye, Mr. MicL." I waved over my shoulder and went to find my room.

An Uneasy Truth 2

That was extremely odd. I wanted to curse his ass out and show him how real DC people act but I knew there was a time and a place for everything. I am not sure of his angle but it's way too much that he sat next to me on the flight, now he's in the same hotel on the same floor. This has got to be some sort of set up. My mind immediately darted to all of the bullshit I left back home.

No, I thought, *he's not that smart*. I closed my eyes and took a deep breath. I'm tripping. It's just a side effect of the long ass ride. So, I slowly undressed in front of the large wall mirror. I am a sexy mother-shut yo' mouth. I smiled at my reflection. I'm in Paris and no one is going to ruin this high. I tossed my clothes on the floor and stepped into the large bathroom.

It was pearly white with a huge walk in shower. I turned the water up as high as it would go and started to wash the airport smell off. After a long shower, I wrapped myself in one of the large plush towels and sat on the edge of the king sized bed. Flipping through the hotel guide, I stared at the room service menu. There was a whole list of shit I couldn't pronounce and the pictures made it worst. I picked up the phone and ordered what looked like a burger. As I waited for my food, a knock came to the door. Still dressed in only a towel, I looked through the peephole, expecting to see MicL. Surprisingly though, the courier with my luggage and Truth was right behind him. I opened the door and stepped aside so he'd have room to slide the carrousel into the room.

"Thank you very much." I smiled.

"Have you had the opportunity to exchange your currency madam?"

"Oh shit," I snapped my teeth. "I knew there was something I was forgetting."

"Don't fret, darling. The exchange is downstairs. Visit when you're fit." He stepped out and closed the door.

"I see you found me." I said to Truth as she walked around admiring my room.

"Of course I did, unfortunately you may not see much of me unless it's the runway the receptionist gave me the itinerary sent over by the modeling agency." She said in a down tone.

"Aww damn cuz, that's okay. At least were flying back together." I said trying to put a bandage on the boo boo.

"I know right. Shit this is the designer I have a fitting for in a few minutes let me run. Love you and I'll text you." Truth said checking her cellphone before kissing Isis on the cheek and running out the door.

"Damn, I'm glad I'm not a model." I laughed to myself, the lifestyle seemed to demanding and out of your own control.

Moments later room service arrived. I was completely disappointed, though. Whatever I ordered was surely not a burger. It smelled like horse ass and looked like a slab of shit. I tooted my nose up and plopped down on the bed.

"This is some straight bullshit." My stomach started growling and I was getting aggravated.

An Uneasy Truth 2

Someone else was at the damn door so, I jumped up and threw a robe on. This time it was MicL. I snapped my teeth and snatched the door open.

"Yes?"

"I was wondering if you were hungry, but it looks like you've already gotten some room service." He pointed.

I looked over my shoulder and laughed, "That shit is horrible."

"I know this spot with a little bit more American food, if you wanna join me."

"Let me get dressed. I will meet you down stairs in 15 minutes." I told him, closing the door.

MicL was waiting downstairs in a plaid button up and ripped jeans. He had a black sweater tied around his neck and wore a pair of glasses. I was clad in a simple blue dress and a pair of pumps. I went to the counter to exchange my currency and then, we were off to a small, neatly tucked restaurant. I couldn't wait to eat some French fries and chicken wings. I sipped on a strawberry margarita while MicL slurped down a beer.

"Maybe after this we will go dancing." He suggested. "These people really know how to party."

"Oh really?" I asked. "I wouldn't mind that."

"Sure, you wouldn't." he smiled. "I think you're a really nice girl."

"And you're not too bad yourself but you scare me a little."

"Scare you, how?" he asked.

I looked down at the tray of fries and said, "I don't know."

"Well, I don't bite; unless you want me too."

I looked up at him and laughed. We enjoyed the rest of the dinner and then went to a club, I swear I thought I was going to suffocate. These people don't wear deodorant so it smelled like a bag of musky old men. I tried my best not to gag and took back four shots of tequila. I was dancing and having such a good time that I couldn't really smell anything by the end of the night. MicL held on to my waist as we slow danced to some song. I was really feeling myself. When we got back to the hotel, he walked me to my room and kissed me on the cheek.

"Thanks. I had a good time." I looked into his sparkly brown eyes.

"Me, too," he touched the small of my back.

I hadn't been caressed like that since Troy made love to me. My heart was pounding in my chest and I leaned in to kiss him on the lips. His mouth opened a little and I sucked on his bottom lip. I pulled away and nervously chuckled.

"Wanna come in?" I asked, opening the room door. The shots and margaritas were truly having their way with me.

"Yeah." MicL answered, following me inside.

He pushed me down on the bed and laid in between my legs as he pushed my panties to the side. His tongue explored my mouth and his hands danced about my body. I moaned in his ear as he tickled my clitoris. I was getting hot and ready. I wrapped my legs around his back and bit him on the neck.

"You want me?" he asked.

"Yes," I purred like a cat in heat.

He pulled away and dropped his pants. Lord have mercy! It was not a big dick but it wasn't small, either. It was rock hard though. I bit my bottom lip and pulled my dress over my head.

"You got a condom?" I asked him.

"Uh," he stuttered. "I..."

"No, glove, no love." I shook my head and crawled to the other side of the bed. I pulled out my wallet and grabbed one that I had in there. "Now, Mr. Cool you should know better than to be walking around unprotected." I scolded.

"You're right," he snatched the condom and quickly put it on.

By then, I was sprawled out on the bed, my fingers rubbing against my juicy pussy. He leaned down on the bed and slowly put himself inside of me. I was shaking a little bit—I'm not sure if I was nervous or just plain horny. It had been a while since I had been with a man but I wanted to be fucked. After all, I am in France.

After a few rounds of sex, I laid tangled in MicL's sheets. "How the fuck did we end up over here?" I thought to myself, He was beside me, snoring. I smiled. I still got it.

I slowly pulled back the covers and climbed out of bed, trying not to wake him. I quickly put on my clothes and slid out of his room. Once I was back in my suite, I pulled out my phone to check my messages. My lips curled up at a hasty message on my voicemail. I tossed the phone and shrugged my shoulders. Not the time or the place. I took a shower and laid down in the bed until a knock startled me.

"Yes," I asked cautiously approaching the door. "Who is it?"

"Room service."

I frowned, opening the door. "I didn't…"

"Mr. MicL asked us to bring this over for you." A woman said, pushing a cart of food and Red wine into the room. "Enjoy." She smiled, her hand out for a tip. I gave her a few dollars and closed the door behind her.

"Whatever it is, it sure smells good." I smiled uncovering what looked like a rack of lamb. "Who's supposed to eat all of this?" I grabbed the of Red wine and poured a cup.

Then, the phone rang. "May I join you?" MicL asked on the other end.

"Oh, I thought you were out for the night." I chuckled.

He laughed and said, "You sure did put it on me."

"Don't I know it." I smiled.

"Well, can I join you?" he asked again.

"Of course, Mr. Cool."

A few minutes later, he was sitting at the table next to me. He hooked an iPhone to the Bluetooth radio in the room and played some old school R&B. I damned sure didn't come to Paris to fall in love, but Mr. Cool was surely winning some brownie points. I watched him out of the corner of my eye as he dipped a strawberry in chocolate. He brought it to my mouth and I obliged. Damn this man is fine.

"Umm," I moaned, taking a bite.

"Bitter huh? Nothing like back home."

"Nope," I shook my head. "Sometimes I miss home but then, I am glad to be away." I shared. "There was way too much going on in my life back home."

"Like?"

"No, it's too long of a story. It would bore you." I shook my head.

"We've got nothing but time, baby girl." MicL touched my thigh.

"All I want to do is get away from it," I put my hand on his shoulder and our eyes locked.

He leaned in and kissed me. I leaned away, "MicL…"

"Sweetheart?"

"I don't…"

He sat back in his seat and sighed. He looked kind of disappointed and he hadn't even heard me out.

"I was going to say, I wanted to wait until after we've eaten this food," I burst into laughter. "You over there looking like a sad little puppy.

"Girl, you got too many tricks up your sleeves."

I cut my eyes at him. "Tricks? Who you calling a trick?"

He threw his hands up. "Isis, chill."

"Yeah…Okay…" I grinned and shook my head, picking up a spoonful of mashed potatoes.

Suddenly, my stomach was rumbling, and I felt like I had to shit. I jumped up from the table and ran into the bathroom. "Oh my God," I leaned over the toilet and threw up.

MicL knocked on the door and said, "Isis are you okay?"

"I…" I pressed my head on the wall, "I don't know. What the hell were we eating? My stomach is all types of fucked up."

"It's pork something or another." He said.

My eyes got big. "Oh my god!" I threw up again. "I don't eat pork."

"I'm sorry. Can I get you something?"

"There are some pain pills in my bag and Pepto." I told him.

MicL fumbled around in the room. "Damn, girl, you got some of everything up in here."

Fuck my entire life! I was sitting in the middle of the bathroom with my head in the toilet while a stranger rummaged through my stuff. I stood up from the floor and opened the door, sticking my hand out. MicL placed two Tylenols and Pepto Bismo in my hand.

"Thanks. Please leave."

"No," he responded. "I'll stay here to make sure you're alright."

"Suite yourself. I have to shit so bad." I closed the door and damn near fell off the side of the toilet trying to hurry up and sit down.

I have never been more humiliated in my life. When I came out the bathroom, MicL had made himself comfortable on the sofa. He was watching Love and Basketball, one of my favorite movies. I sat down next to him with a refreshed look on my face.

"Feeling better?"

"Don't go to the bathroom for about forty-five minutes and we'll be cool."

We laughed. My stomach was starting to settle. He had taken the liberty to have the food out of the room, too. I leaned back on the couch and tried not to think about anything. The movie seemed to be watching us because when I opened my eyes, MicL was asleep and the movie was just about over. I was going to wake him but decided against it and got up to go to bed.

There was a lot I needed to do the next day to get ready for the show. I'm sure I was snoring when I finally went to sleep but I was awakened by a soft nudge.

"Isis?"

"Huh?"

"I'm gone. I will see you in the morning." MicL kissed me on the forehead.

"Just don't feed me any more pork." I mumbled before turning over.

***

The next morning, I met MicL downstairs for the complimentary breakfast. He was sitting in the corner of the dining hall reading a newspaper. He had shaved but he only wore a t-shirt and basketball shorts.

"So, you are from DC, huh?" I as I sat down at his table referring to his morning attire. He lowered the newspaper.

"You've got jokes, Shitty."

My mouth dropped with embarrassment, but I laughed anyway. At least my stomach wasn't hurting anymore. I thought for sure that I had food poisoning. I shook my head and looked around to see what they were serving for breakfast. I half ass wanted to eat it. On one hand, I couldn't afford to be sick in Paris and on the other, I was hungry as hell. The only thing I recognized was the turkey bacon, but I was surprised they knew to serve it. I piled my plate with a couple of slices and poured a glass of orange juice.

An Uneasy Truth 2

"You good?" MicL asked, still browsing the paper.

"Yea," I nodded.

"Cool."

We sat there in silence while I finished my breakfast. I got a text from Professor Stewart with the address for where we'd be meeting up to get our looks together for the show. I was getting excited all over again. I knew that the skills I had were enough to get my family out of DC forever; at this point to give up stripping and selling rocks it was all I ever dreamed up. This trip was make it or break it. I was determined to make a name for myself despite what lead me here while I'm here. So, I went upstairs and gathered everything I needed. MicL said that his meeting was on the other side of town and he hoped to see me later that evening. Knowing my professor though, I wasn't expecting to be back at the hotel until sunrise.

There were three models assigned to me. One was almost as dark as midnight, one was chubby, and the other was as thin as a piece of cardstock paper. I already envisioned what I could do to enhance them, to make them stand out.

"Hey, I'm K Secret." One of the other designers reached for a hand shake.

I looked down at her hand and replied, "Isis."

She frowned and mumbled, "Well, nice to meet you too."

I was trying not to be rude but I was Focused so I took a swig of the Brandy Professor Stewart had sitting at each station. I was going to get nice. *Hell*, I thought, *I should have smoked a blunt*. I picked out the materials I was going to be using to make some of my designs as well as the hair for each girl. I started with the chocolate one. She was a representation of me, so she had to be on point in every part of the fashion show I came to win this shit. When I walk away everyone will know my name.

After hours of working, all I wanted to do was crash at the hotel. I put a do not disturb sign on the door and picked up my phone. I checked my social sites to make sure that things were still calm back home. I was kind of missing that place, but I had to push all of that to the side. I wasn't worrying about none of them half-lives. I just wanted my kids to have better. It had been hard enough raising them on my own, but I knew that fashion was better than stripping and dealing on any day of the week. Their faces were my motivation.

I placed my phone on the night stand and plugged it into the charger and turned on the television. Hell, even the TV stations are whack, I thought as I scrolled. Then, Joseline of Love and Hip Hop popped up. I smiled.

"Yesss!" I leaned back on the head board and took a sip of a soda. I was all ears for some ghetto-fide drama.

After all designers were stitched and fitted to the proper models it seemed like time sped up because everything went so fast I hadn't realized I had been to Paris until I got home. Apparently Imajean collection was killing the runways of Paris, Jon Marc was doing their thing too leaving blood on the runway and the line I worked on Royalty Reigns all got great reviews. After I got home I never heard from Mr.Cool again guess one of those case where what happens there stays there.

Chapter 12

It was the third night back from Paris and I still had jet lag. Needless to say, I really didn't want to be bothered so Mommy and Daddy Lo had the kids for the week. I jumped in a nice hot bubble bath and turned the radio to 93.9. I loved their evening mix and suddenly breaking news a woman found murdered in Anacostia park she was identified as Summore Right. Police have arrested Antonio Blackmon for her murder.

"Black and Summore?" I said aloud as I dried off my fingertips a dialed Cita.

She picked up on the first ring.

"I take it you got the news." Cita said.

"So, it's who I think it is, for real?" I asked now taking in the news.

"Yup, word on the street is they were arguing outside Club Spread and he shoved her in his car and pulled off." Cita said. She only knew of Black through Isis when he came by the Club from time to time but Summore got what she had coming.

"Damn you mean to tell me that bitch Summore was living a reckless life under her real name? Silly bitch." I said to myself as I sat back in the tub.

"I know right? I heard about what they cooked up for you and Troy while you were missing in action she had that shit coming I only came to Club Spread because I heard this where she been hiding, Oh I was gonna take care of that for you sis." Cita said as she inhaled the weed smoke meaning every word.

"Thanks girl. Well let me enjoy my bath I'll be in contact." I said before hanging up.

I sent a group chat to Cita, Charli, Truth, Melanie, Mahogany, Destiny and Shell we needed to get together for a lady's night. After everyone agreed on meeting up on my birthday the upcoming weekend at Country Inn and Suites in Capital heights right off the beltway, I finally stood and showered before getting out and rubbing cocoa butter all over my skin I slept in nothing and like a baby.

Ring …

"Hello." Mel answered his cellphone

"Uncle Mel you should really get over here." VJ said in a shaky tone.

"What's going on Nephew?" Mel asked as he stepped away from the background chatter to hear him clearly.

"I shot my mom I think she's dead, Can you come?" VJ said nervously

"I'm on my way." Mel said before hanging up.

"Ma-ma and Mel ride with me." He said as he jetted out of the door and straight to his car, by the time the twins got outside he was pulling up in front of them, they got in and Mel sped off.

"What's up Mel? And slow the fuck down I got my pistol on me." Melanie asked

"I don't know we will find out when we pull up." Mel said as his mind did numbers he was silently praying VJ didn't do what he called and said he did.

Mel parked and ran inside with Mahogany and Melanie on his heels he tapped on the door and VJ let them in when he saw Valerie's legs sprawled on the floor from the kitchen he just shook his head in disbelief.

"I'm already calling Smurf." Melanie said as she stepped away.

"Why VJ?" Mel asked while Mahogany silently thought of why she deserved it and if Mel knew he wouldn't even care probably would dap him up and keep it pushing.

"Does it matter? Put him in the car and let's go." Mahogany said ready to leave, she was kind of irritated she hadn't got to pull the trigger.

"I'mma take you to Destiny, don't tell nobody you did this do you understand me?" Mel said looking VJ in his eyes, he could see that VJ was very nonchalant as if he had plucked a roach.

Suddenly a gurgling cough came from the kitchen, Mel took VJ outside and Melanie was in the bathroom, Mahogany's eyes lit up like she hit the lottery as she stood over a struggling Valerie to breathe she crotched down next to her grabbed her windpipe and twisted it killing her instantly.

"That was for my little sister." Mahogany said with an evil grin before standing up and walking outside to the car. Melanie came out of the bathroom looking around "Oh hell nahhh." She mumbled when she noticed they left her in the apartment before she walked outside, and they left.

"VJ where did you get a pistol from anyway?" Melanie asked turning around to face him from the front seat.

"It was my mom's I heard her talking on the phone about how the chicks she paid to murk Isis couldn't get the job done." He replied shaking his head from side to side.

"Who taught you to shoot then?" Mel asked now very interested to know who taught what has up until this point been a pretty square kid to kill.

"My brother. I know what I did was wrong, but she has lied to me all my life and my father too Isis has been so nice to me and more of a mother than her." VJ said with his head hung low.

Mahogany reached over and hugged him she knew exactly what he was feeling she too shot and killed her own mother. "Sometimes we have to make decisions that others won't understand son." She said honestly to him while hugging him.

A few months went by and surprisingly drama had died. Destiny and Mel were an item, Nadine and Loco were stronger than ever he even stepped out the drug life leaving everything with Smurf, Shell and Tate hooked back up his loyalty couldn't be denied and they loved each other like no other, Melanie and Mahogany still in the murder game even putting Mel on a few jobs, Lem, Sky, VJ and Jahmier all started middle school together causing havoc to anybody that crossed the four, Black got convicted of Summore's murder he said "it was an accident but hey they had a deal" was all he said to the judge before sentencing.

It was Ladies night the girls decided to meet up at country inn and suites in capital heights. They all met in the lobby and headed to the suite. It was huge with a king sized bed, a full kitchen, Jacuzzi and pull out sofa in an adjacent room. All the girls began to chat and get comfortable while Isis made drinks in the blender.

"Drinks Ladies." She announced as she sat all the champagne flutes on the bar top.

TAP TAP TAP. Melanie answered the door.

"Heyy I'm Destiny, is Isis here?" Destiny asked as she stepped inside with her overnight bag.

"Oh my god D! Look at you!" Isis said as she skipped over and hugged Destiny admiring her hair that wasn't in its naturally curly state anymore it was now bone straight one half Blackest of black and the other side a rich bright red.

"Oh, you did that mu'fucka lil sis. You gotta give me your stylist number." Shell said admiring Destiny's hair. She and Destiny had become very close since Destiny and Mel became an item.

"I sure will. Ok where my drink it's Isis Birthday!!" Destiny said as she walked over to the kitchen sitting a bottle of 1800 on the counter.

An Uneasy Truth 2

"Ooo yes I can definitely use a drink after the past couple weeks I've been having with Leo." Truth said as she took as sip of the frozen strawberry lime Margarita Isis made.

"I second that emotion." Charli said referring to her boyfriend Ali.

"I see the first topic of discussion is these fucked up niggas." Shell said grabbing her drink and having a seat on the sofa. All the girls got their snacks and drinks and gathered around for some girl talk. By 2 am they were all drunk and had passed out all over the room.

The next morning, they rotated the shower and made breakfast while they got to know each other better. It was a good vibes and when it was time to go everyone decided to meet back up in a few weeks.

Chapter 13

"Why the fuck can't I go with you? I go any other time. This is some bullshit and you brand new tonight! Oh, since you recruited some new bitches, all of a sudden I can't go?" Charli ranted as Ali continued to get dressed nonchalantly.

"Damn! The first time I say no is like I never said yes," Ali quoted Destiny's Child song jokingly as he sat on the end of their king-sized sleigh bed putting on his Foamposite's. He laughed at her tantrums because they didn't faze him. They had been together six years on and off. "I'll just take her little ass shopping tomorrow, then she'll get over it," he said to himself as he smoothed out his fresh black tee and adjusted his belt in his dark blue Antik denim jeans. He stepped back and gave his outfit the once over in the large, full-length mirror that hung on the bedroom wall. He threw on his black fitted cap and headed towards their bedroom door to leave, tuning out any other comments Charli had to throw his way.

"I'm focused on this money, young, so you will not be taking me out my character," Ali thought to himself. He knew that if he bothered entertaining the argument even with a comment as small as that, Charli would go ape shit. A smile crept across his face as he thought about the new chicks he hired a few days ago, Cherry and Mystique. Ali quickly scooped up his keys and cell off the nightstand and started in the direction of the bedroom door.

"Oh, you got jokes mu'fucka?" Charli said through clenched teeth as she launched a glass that had been sitting nearby on the night stand. Ali stopped in his tracks when he saw the glass shatter on the wall missing him by inches.

An Uneasy Truth 2

He smoothly turned to face Charli. "Damn ma, your aim off tonight. Love you, I'm out." He laughed as he continued out the door.

Charlie got out of bed pissed as she paced the plush area rug in their bedroom. Ali's "I don't give a fuck" attitude wasn't new to her, however, lately he had been 10 times worse and extremely reckless. She dealt with the two-day disappearing acts knowing he was with any one of the thirsty bitches he fucked with at the club, but she felt like as long as it didn't come home then she wasn't tripping. See, most females would've hung it up said "fuck this relationship and fuck dude too", and Charli did until something brought them back together.

Charli walked over to the window and watched as Ali drove out of the parking lot. "This mu'fucka want to play," she thought out loud. She walked through the hall of her apartment into her spacious living room and picked up her cell phone off the charger noticing she had three text messages. She touched the screen to retrieve them. The first was from Khalil, Ali's right-hand man and her homie and the second was from Kandy, Ali's niece who looked up to Charli.

She bypassed those two when saw the 187 texts from her cousin, Truth. "Oh, my gee, what the fuck Joe?" was the only thought repeatedly running through her head as she rushed down the hall and into her room to change her clothes. After listening to all that Shell an Isis went through and now a 187 text from Truth my life is feeling like a movie." Charli thought to herself.

She grabbed a pair of black cargo joggers, black timberlands and a plain black tee. "187... 187... 187..." she repeated to herself as she rushed back through the living room, grabbing her keys and cell on her way out of the door. She hit the auto start as she jogged down the sidewalk to her royal blue tinted Lincoln Town Car.

"Damn, fine fucking time to be parked so far from this damn building," she fussed making her way to her car, running out of breath. She jumped into the driver's seat and sped off. Charli called Truth on speaker and after a few unanswered tries she finally answered.

"Bitch, there's somebody in here. I'm in the downstairs bathroom. Hurry," Truth whispered in a calm tone.

"I'm doing 65 to you, baby. Seven minutes flat," Charli said before hanging up and racing to her cousin's house to save the day... once again. "Some shit just doesn't change," Charli thought to herself as she tapped in the security code of her hidden compartment, retrieved her Glock .45 and placed it on her lap as she turned onto Truth street. As Charli cautiously crept up to Truth's door, she noticed it had been kicked in.

"Who the fuck kicked in your door?" Charli thought to herself as she slowly walked through the door, firmly gripping her pistol. She heard movement coming from upstairs, so she decided against going up there. She didn't know how many intruders she would be facing. Charli crept to the bathroom near the back of Truth's house, and lightly tapped on the door and whispered "Blood." It had been she and Truth's code word since they were kids. Instantly, the door opened, and she was snatched inside the bathroom.

"Oh, my gee, I'm so...," Truth began to whisper as she hugged her cousin tight.

An Uneasy Truth 2

"Bitch, shut the fuck up, you loaded?" Charli cut her off.

"Ummm... Ummm... I don't know, fuck, I think so," Truth whispered nervously as she searched the bathroom and found the loaded .22 Leo kept stashed for situations like this.

"But... but I need to tell you..." Truth began again but Charli cut her off. "Fuck that, let's go," she said through gritted teeth as they slowly exited the bathroom.

"Charli, I really need to tell you something," Truth whispered as she nervously gripped the .22 and slowly walked behind Charli.

Truth had bust a gun before, but it wasn't exactly what she preferred. She hated conflict. Even as a youngin', her battles were fought by Charli, her sister, Nadia or her brother, Jon. Not that she couldn't, because she could hold her own. Truth was pretty and prissy. She stood 5 feet 8 inches and 185lbs. that were perfectly proportioned with smooth, mocha skin and rust colored doe-like eyes. She was very beautiful. She kept some bait which unfortunately kept her mixed up in some bullshit.

"Did you hear me, Cha?" Truth whispered.

"Shhh," Charli replied as she stopped in the darkness of the hallway.

Truth followed closely behind Charli down the dark hall as set of footsteps came down the stairs. The TV was on in the living room illuminating a portion of the stairway area. As the footsteps got closer to the bottom of the stairs, a figure became visible, giving Charli and Truth the upper hand because they were able to see the intruders and not be seen.

"Mann, Truth always got some shit going on. My heart doesn't pump Kool-Aid so this mu'fucka coming down these steps better be on point," Charli thought to herself. She prepared to pump slugs into the intruder, gripping the handle of her .45 tight and trying to tune Truth's ass out.

"BOOM!" a shot rang off instantly snapping Charli out of her thoughts. Neither Charli nor Truth moved or made sound as they watched and listened to the two intruders.

"You stupid bitch!" a female voiced yelled out in pain.

"Oh my god! Oh my god! Oh my god! Kasey, I'm so sorry," Kima said as she rushed over to help her friend Kasey as she began to fall to the floor.

"What the fuck, man? This shit hurts! Shoot first and ask questions later, right?" Kasey said as she doubled over in pain. She looked down, noticing her black hoodie was becoming soaked in her blood. Blood was now flowing; just not from whom she intended, which was Truth.

"I got to get you help. I'm so sorry," Kima said with panic dripping from her voice. She threw Kasey's arm over her shoulder and ushered her out the open door toward her black Chevy Tahoe.

"Bitch, I'ma die, but I guess that's karma because I came to get Slim out of my way," Kasey said through coughs as Kima pushed her into the backseat.

An Uneasy Truth 2

"Don't say that, Kasey. I'ma get you help," Kima said as she hurried around to the driver side jumped in and sped off.

"Shiiiiiid, that was close, huh cuz?" Truth said with a sigh of relief.

"Bitch!" Charli yelled as she punched her in the arm, giving her a frog. "We could've been blasted on or even worse, killed! Tell me what the fuck is going on now!" she said, looking at Truth through squinted eyes. Her hand was on her curvy hip, still gripping her pistol at her side.

Truth was thrown off slightly. She stood there, still rubbing her arm. She knew Charli wasn't a game and the anger on her face said it all. Charli was cool, but she didn't play games. She stood 5 feet 4 inches and 145 lbs. with a smooth chestnut complexion and almond-shaped eyes that accentuated her baby face. Although she was small, she was bossy and what she lacked in size she made up for in attitude and automatic weapons. Truth began to pace back and forth in the hall trying to gather her thoughts.

"Man, Cha. I'm pregnant."

"What? When did you find out? Fuck that, let's go. I'm uncomfortable standing here conversating all Willy-nilly like a bitch ain't just come here to blow your fucking head off," Charli said as she tucked her pistol and headed out the door. Truth followed behind her grabbing her purse and closing the door as best she could on her way out.

***

Charli started her car and turned up the volume on her system and Hail Mary by 2Pac began to play through her speakers.

"Evil lurks, enemies, see me flee

Activate my hate; let it break, to the flame

Set trip, empty out my clip, never stop to aim" 2Pac's voice boomed strong throughout the car as Charli recited the lyrics along with him. Truth climbed in and shut the door then Charli pulled off. 10 minutes into the ride, Charli turned down the music and broke the silence.

"Continue," she said.

"Okay, I just found out I was pregnant tonight. I was in the bathroom and it was like all I saw were those damn pink lines and the tears just poured uncontrollably. That's when the doorbell rang. I figured fuck it. I didn't invite no company and whoever it was should've called first but then it got persistent so as I started to pull my life together and go see who it was, BOOM! I got spooked, jumped in the tub, and texted you, praying you got here," Truth said with dramatics as she went back to rubbing the spot on her arm Charli had punched.

"So, who the fuck want your head, T?" Charli asked in a calm tone.

"I don't know, cuz. This shit is crazy and overwhelming," Truth said, staring into the night sky as she became lost in her thoughts. "Damn, who the fuck is Kasey? I wonder if Charli heard the names...," Truth thought to herself.

An Uneasy Truth 2

Charlie just shook her head from side to side in disbelief and turned the music back up. They continued the ride, both women lost in their thoughts. Charli was wondering how the hell she was going to get her cousin out of this situation while Truth was wondering whose seed she was carrying. Charli jumped on BW Parkway and headed to a cozy little bar named Lucks on Benning Road in Northeast DC. She found herself there when she needed to go missing in action and gather her thoughts. Today was one of those days because this current situation was going to take a lot of thought.

Chapter 14

"You going to be okay, Kasey. Just hold on. We are almost there," Kima said frantically as she pulled into the ambulance entrance of Doctor's Hospital laying on the horn. "Oh my god! Oh my god! HEEELLLLLPP!! My friend has been shot!" Kima screamed at the top of her lungs.

The hospital staff began to rush out with a stretcher. "Okay ma'am, we need you to calm down. The doctors are going to do all they can to help your friend," a male nurse said as they quickly pushed a now unconscious Kasey down the hall to the operating room.

"Please save her, please," Kima cried as she tried to follow them back.

"Okay, okay ma'am. I need you to calm down. They are going to do everything they can to help your friend," a kind young Asian nurse said in a comforting tone as she ushered Kima to the waiting area to have a seat. Kima pulled herself together as much as she could, took a seat, and gave the nurse as much information as she knew about Kasey.

"Okay, this should be good. As soon as they have information, one of the doctors will be out to give you an update, okay?" Lisa said as she stood up to walk away.

"Okay thank you, umm, Lisa?" Kima asked, trying to read Lisa's nametag through her tears.

An Uneasy Truth 2

"Yes. You're very welcome," Lisa said before walking away to tend to her duties. Kima rushed out to her truck and moved it to a parking space. She picked up her cell and dialed the only person she could talk to and calm her nerves. Kima sat and called back to back as her nerves raced a mile a minute. Ring... ring... ring...

"Hello," the male voice finally picked up after ignoring the call four times.

"King, I need you," Kima nervously said through the receiver.

"Kima, what's wrong?" He asked, sensing the uneasy tone in her voice.

"Can you meet me at Doctor's Hospital, please?" She said as tears began to stream down her face.

"Kima, is Amina okay?" King asked feeling uneasy about the call.

"Yes, she is fine. Just come, please. I need you," Kima said

"Aight, ma. I'll be there soon," he said then disconnected the call.

Damn I told Kasey this move was a bad idea. I didn't mean to shoot her. I got jumpy, FUCK!

Kima sat quietly in the silence of her truck as the scene replayed in her head. Kima and Kasey had been friends since third grade. They always felt more like sisters than best friends. Kima's mom, Anita, and Kasey's mom, Tiffany, were neighbors in the same apartment building. Tiffany had just gotten back custody of Kasey by the time she was in third grade. Anita and Gerald, Kasey's dad, had a fling and Kasey was created in the heat of passion. Gerald broke things off by the time Kasey was three and sued Anita for custody of Kasey. Anita fought to keep Kasey, however, between lawyer and court fees, everyday survival, and taking care of Kasey, Anita loss her apartment, car, job and most importantly, Kasey.

Gerald was awarded custody and although it caused his wife to go ballistic, she accepted Kasey and treated her as her own. Anita fell into a depression feeling like the only thing she actually had to live for was ripped away. Having no family and no one to turn to, she tried to commit suicide and was admitted for 6 months. With the psychological help she needed, she recovered quickly. Within a year, she got back on her grind, doing anything and everything she could to get on back on her feet. Anita checked into the shelter at DC general and began to network with people to better herself. Tiffany worked as a counselor at the shelter. Anita walked into her office, explained her situation, and Tiffany helped her.

Since that moment, they became thick as thieves. Tiffany helped her find employment with a cleaning company and even called in a favor at the Department of Social Services and got a Section 8 certificate and got her a cozy little one-bedroom apartment with a den. They were ecstatic to find out that Anita's apartment was one building down from her and her daughter. She genuinely cared about Anita and wanted to see that she got her daughter back. She couldn't imagine being in that same situation and losing her daughter, Kima. In the process, they became very close. Anita took all the required steps to get Kasey back in the eyes of the courts.

An Uneasy Truth 2

She even saved some money and began to flip it by buying ounces and selling small packages to the clients she cleaned for. A few months later, she had stacked her savings to a comfortable amount and furnished her apartment. Tiffany was proud of Anita's progress but had no knowledge of Anita's side hustle. By the time Kasey was in the second grade, Anita had begun the process of getting her back and won two months before Kasey entered third grade. Kasey and Kima we introduced and clicked instantly. It was like they had both found the sister they each longed for after being only children.

It became rare that you would see Kima without Kasey until middle school when Anita got locked up on drug trafficking charges and Kasey was sent back to her father in Largo. As fate would have it, Kima was on the train and she and Kasey ran into each other. They were so happy to see each other. They hugged and caught up as much as possible during the train ride and exchanged numbers, promising to link up and that weekend they did.

Kima was snapped out of her daze by King tapping on the window. She felt a sense of relief wash over her once she got out and was secure within his warm embrace.

"What's going on?" he asked as he stepped back to examine her. "Whose fucking blood is on you?" he questioned further, noticing the smeared blood on her grey hoodie.

"It's Kasey's," she said in a whisper as tears began to flood her face.

"Get in the truck," he instructed as he walked around and got in the passenger seat.

"Goddamn, Kima. That's all her blood too?" he asked once he got in and saw the backseat.

"Man, yea. This shit is horrible. I didn't mean to shoot her, King. I swear it was an accident." Kima cried as she shook nervously. He reached over and hugged her.

"Damn, I hate to see her like this. Wait, what the fuck did she just say?" he thought to himself as what Kima said registered in his brain.

"Wait. What the fuck you mean you didn't mean to shoot her?" King asked as he pulled her away to look into her eyes.

"It was Kasey's idea to…"

"Man, Kima. Please don't tell me you were with a dumb Kasey move and this is the end result," he asked thru clenched teeth. Kima just nodded her head yes, knowing he saw right thru her so lying wasn't an option.

"See man, this bullshit got to cease. Ever since you hooked up with shawty, you been mixed up in some bullshit. Tell me what the fuck happened," he said as he sat back and lit his Newport and listened. Kima knew she had to come up with a lie a good one since there was no way she could tell him they were at Leo's house and that the bullet was actually meant for Leo's girl.

"Well a few weeks ago, me and Kasey got into it with some chicks from uptown. Kasey came up with the idea we should catch them unexpected when they thought we forgot. We got to fighting and shit went wrong and instead of shooting the girl in the tussle, I shot Kasey by accident," she lied as she fumbled with Kasey's cell phone. Not once did she look up to make eye with King. She was praying he didn't pick up on the bullshit she was laying on him. King instantly picked up on the bullshit she was telling him, but he just remained cool and put his Newport out.

"Aye, Kima. Whatever you do, keep in mind you got my daughter out here to look after. You need to dismiss that Team Ride or Die bullshit with Kasey. She ain't got shit to live for so she rides to die but you do. But I love you, be safe, and call me if you need me, and clean up this fucking truck." King said in a disappointed tone as he got out, not giving Kima a chance to respond.

***

"I'm sorry I involved you. I didn't have anybody else I could call," Truth said as tears began to well up in her eyes.

"We family, cuz. You did the right thing. Don't worry, we will figure out who wants your head and who dat baby pappy is." Charli said jokingly, trying to lighten the mood. She parked, and they walked into the bar. A handsome older gentleman was tending the bar.

"Hey stranger," Mack greeted with a warm smile.

"Hey, Mack." Charli smiled at her old friend.

Mack was in his late 50's, tall, dark, fit, and handsome. He had a positive aura about him that people loved to be around.

"What will you and beautiful be having tonight? Mack asked, smiling at Truth.

"Two double shots of henny please," Charli replied, laughing at Mack's flirting with Truth.

"Gotchu love, and these rounds are on the house," Mack said as he stepped away to pour the shots.

"See that's what gets you in the position you in now," Charli whispered to Truth. As she laughed it was as if the smile had been sucked out of Truth's face.

"See Cha, that's not funny," Truth said pouting playfully, causing them both to erupt in laughter.

Mack brought the shots over and Charli downed them both back to back while they chatted back and forth watching the football game that was playing on one of the many 50-inch flat screens throughout the bar.

"Still like sports huh?" a male voice asked after about twenty minutes and 2 more shots later.

Charli did not hear him; however, Truth took the initiative to turn around and see who was talking. As she looked into the gentleman's eyes, her heart started to beat rapidly. Not out of romance, but sheer shock. The words she wanted to say formed in her head but for some reason wouldn't roll off her tongue, nor was she able to move a muscle. She had heard about Supreme but had never met him. Supreme reached over and lifted Truth's chin, closing her mouth. She smiled bashfully.

"You still think you can whoop my ass in Madden?"

Charli turned in Truth's direction and noticed the look in her cousin's eyes. They read surprise. She focused in on the hand that was now moving away from Truth's chin. Charli's eyes followed the arm until she reached the face. The moment their eyes connected, her heart exploded into tiny butterflies began to flutter inside her stomach. "Sssupreme," she said, jumping off the barstool excitedly and wrapping her arms around his neck and hugging him tightly.

"Sup, Star," he laughed, calling her the nickname he gave her and returning the warm embrace.

"Oh, my gee! When did you get home? How did you know it was me? What are you doing here?" Charli rambled question after question, excited to see her old friend and love.

Truth sat quietly. She was tipsy with a smile on her face and just glad to see some happiness in the day. She was still keeping in mind that she needed to find out who Kasey was and why she was on her hit list.

Chapter 15

*T*ake it off bitch bend over let me see it. I'm sweet James Jones and a trick I couldn't be it... Pimp C's verse from "Let Me See" it blared through the loud speakers of Club Spread. Ali's veteran dancer, Luscious, was working the stage in an indigo blue bikini with glow in the dark stars and a pair of 6-inch clear stilettos with an ankle strap that had indigo tint. She had lustful eyes molesting every inch of her ass and she loved every minute of it. The eyes followed her as she climbed up the pole located in the center of the stage and flipped upside down and slid down with her legs spread wide. The stage was covered in bills of all denominations. Luscious knew how to give a good show. She had been dancing for Ali for about 4 years, way before he had a club.

The other scantily clad ladies sashayed throughout the club greeting everyone who entered. Ali's gentleman's club, Club Spread, stayed on jump ever since he opened its doors a year ago. Three months ago, he agreed to house open mic events every Monday, Thursday, and Saturday night with two of his closest friends, AK and Kazi. The nights were profitable, and the live musical entertainment was enjoyed by everyone.

It was a Thursday night. Ali had just pulled into the parking lot near the corner where he could view all activity, admiring the turn out. It was only 9:30 and the line was trailing down the walkway of the club and into the parking lot. Damn, Kazi was not joking when he said club promo has been serious, he thought to himself with a grin, noticing

An Uneasy Truth 2

the parking lot was about sixty five percent full which meant revenue was looking good.

AK, Kazi, and Ali all grew up in the same areas all their lives. It seemed like when one family moved, the other two were not far behind from Landover to Southeast DC then back to Landover. In that order, from youth to their teenage years, they had pretty much been inseparable. After high school, they each carved their own paths. They caught up twice a week to discuss business or just to chill they never lost touch. AK took his path toward the drug game. He was raised by a single mother who worked two jobs to support him and his younger brother, Kasiim.

AK didn't know his father and didn't care to know if he was dead or alive. As far as he was concerned, he was dead. Kasiim's dad was killed by a dirty cop in a drug deal gone bad before he was born so to him AK was the only dad he knew, and he treated him with that much respect. AK made sure he attended school, behaved and obeyed their mother while he was not around; he always left his ruthless street business in the street he was determined to keep Kasiim on a straight path. Just looking at AK's 5'8", 160 lbs. frame, smooth, copper skin tone, and chinky eyes, combined with his charm and mannerism, you wouldn't think of him as the intimidating type. But he actually was, especially if it had anything to do with his family. The man will go ape shit.

Kazi on the other hand had that "I'll fuck you up" look written all over him standing 6'4", 315 lbs. of pure, dark chocolate muscle with chestnut colored eyes that showed off his no nonsense demeanor. His presence put people on pins and needles. Unlike AK, his path carried him to college where he majored in advertising and marketing. He also took audio engineering classes where he earned an internship at a local radio station. By the time he was 23, he had stacked enough paper investing funds on the street with AK and built two recording studios called Hood Related Entertainment. One was located on Wilson Blvd. in VA and the other on H Street northeast DC.

***

Tap tap tap...

A light tap broke Ali's thoughts. He looked up to see Juicy, a young, pretty, brown skinned woman that worked the street for Ali, standing there with a smile.

"Get in," he said.

Ali watched as Juicy walked around to the passenger side of the car and got in. Juicy grew up with Ali. She was built like a stallion and she put her sex game down, but her mentality was broken. Ali saw her potential, groomed her, and put her on the market since she was giving it away for free. Juicy reached in her boot and handed him a roll of dollar bills. Ali took the money and stuck it in the center armrest then reached into his pants and pulled out his now hardened tool. Her eyes became bright and full of life. Juicy loved to suck and fuck, especially with Ali.

"Do something with that," he said smoothly as he leaned his seat back, giving Juicy full access to do as requested.

"Damn whatever happened to hello nigga," she laughed as she lowered her head into his lap, taking his thick tool into her warm, wet mouth. Once between her lips, it was like somebody hit the switch on a Hoover Vacuum because her suction game was serious. Her head bobbed up and down with a steady rhythm. Ali couldn't hold it as he felt his nut building up. Juicy felt his wood slightly jump in her mouth indicating he was ready to explode. He grabbed her head as he released his warm baby batter down her throat and she swallowed every drop.

"Take that ass back to work," Ali said with a grin.

"Damn, you just going to rape my mouth, bust your nut, and kick me out," Juicy laughed as she reapplied her lip gloss preparing to get back on the street.

"I do this 'because I can. Who going to stop me?" Ali said as he turned up his music, indicating the conversation was over. Juicy got out and went about her business.

***

Supreme smiled, glad to see his Star had not lost love for him while he was away. He missed her friendship more than anything. When he got locked up, in the beginning she would write, visit, and accept his calls. About year in, it all just stopped. It was as if she did a 180 on him. He didn't understand it, but he accepted it.

"You breathe," he said, laughing at Charli. He then turned around and faced a smiling Truth.

"I apologize for my hand. How you doing, Miss Lady?" he said humbly, extending his hand for her to shake. Truth shook his hand and smiled.

"Oh, I'm just fine. I take it you are Supreme. It's good to finally put a face with a name and story. Trust me, Cha was clearly bout to be on that ass. Did you see that reaction?"

Truth laughed as she tossed back Charli's Henny and Coke. Charli looked at her briefly with the side eye but decided she would address Truth drinking while pregnant once they leave.

"Ha! You know that, though. Supreme, this is my cousin, Truth. Truth, this is Supreme," Charli laughed as she introduced her cousin and her old friend.

"Your ol' late ass. I figured that out on my own, Sherlock. Mack, 3 shots of Henny, please sir," Truth joked as she ordered the three of them a shot. Mack brought them their shots and Truth raised her glass indicating a toast.

"Cheers to reuniting and it feel so gooood," she sang loudly and drunkenly before taking her shot to the head, causing laughter throughout.

Supreme laughed and drank his shot. He took a seat on the bar stool, pulling Charli between his legs to face him and wrapped his arms around her. Damn I've missed you, he thought to himself. He inhaled her scent. Supreme was well aware that Charli and Ali were an item. Though his intentions were not to disrespect their situation, he still felt like Ali didn't deserve her and never did because she was a star. As Charli indulged in Supremes' embrace, old feelings began to flow through her body.

"Well ma, to answer your questions, I came home about eight months ago." Supreme broke the silence. "I work here, so that's what I'm doing here. Mack looked out when I came home, and how could I ever forget my favorite girl?" he said looking into Charli's brown eyes, gently rubbing her smooth cheek with the back of his hand.

An Uneasy Truth 2

"Plus...," he laughed as he spun her around so that her back was now facing him, "You'll never forget me. I see you still got this tattoo," Supreme said jokingly as he kissed the beautiful tat of a sunrise on the back of her neck. Charli smiled as his soft moist lips pressed up against her neck unexpectedly. Truth was in her own world. She had been texting Leo since they left her house to tell him what happened, and he had yet to respond.

Chapter 16

"**Un**-fucking-believable bitches come kicking in our door wanting to blow my head off and this mu'fucka missing in action!" Truth shook her head from side to side, thinking to herself.

"You okay, Miss Lady?" Supreme asked, noticing Truth's change of mood.

"Oh, I'm okay. Thanks," Truth replied throwing on a fake smile and pepping up a bit. "Gotta hit da ladies room. I'll be back real soon," she sang drunkenly as she stumbled a bit while stepping down from the bar stool to make her way to the restroom. A few folks in the bar heard Truth and giggled a bit at her singing.

"Ay, who is driving?" Supreme asked Charli as they both laughed at Truth who had stumbled into a few bar patrons.

"I am...," she replied then paused, "Ummm, Supreme I want to say...," Charli started but he cut her off by gently placing a finger on her lips.

"All I ask of you is that you stay close. Can you do that?" Supreme asked in a sincere tone as he looked into the windows of her soul. Before she could reply, Truth walked up laughing.

An Uneasy Truth 2

"Damnnnnn, bitch. You looking like an open book," Truth said laughing, acknowledging the intense stare between Charli and Supreme.

They both laughed at Truth, and Charli returned her eyes to Supreme's. Although Truth jokingly interjected, she knew Charli's true feelings for him from her feelings for Ali. Supreme held a special place in her heart. He exposed her to real shit while Ali tried to keep her sheltered. Supreme dealt in the drug game while Ali was her drug. For some reason, she couldn't

live without him. Ali and Charli had ups and downs throughout the first year in their relationship, and in that time, she met Supreme. Ali and Charli had a huge falling out about one of his many sideline chicks and she moved out and stayed with Truth and Leo. In that time, she and Supreme got closer and within six months of her leaving Ali, she and Supreme decided to give it a try.

Ali gave her the blues and after a while, it caused drama in Charli and Supreme's situation. Unbeknownst to everyone, the Feds were watching Supreme and wanted to sponsor his lengthy vacation of five years or more to Chesapeake detention facility a super max jail in Baltimore. His lawyers worked diligently and found a technicality, resulting in him only doing three out of the six years before he was released. Ali was content that Supreme was out the picture. He took advantage of the opportunity and slithered his was back into Charli's life as her number one man. He took her shopping and spent money on trips just to take her mind away from the entire situation.

Charli, feeling unhappy and lonely, ended up vulnerable and falling victim to Ali's bullshit and here she was again with her fork in the road. Charli was lost in Supreme's eyes. She felt bad about how things happened, or ended rather, between them. She figured everything happened for a reason as what he just said replayed in her head. "All I ask of you is that you stay close. Can you do that?" She hugged him tight and whispered "I gotchu 'Preme."

After Ali bust his nut and kicked Juicy out, he leaned back in his seat and sparked his pre-rolled Backwood filled with Blue Dream. He took long pulls off the J and could feel himself getting higher with each pull. Damn this shit on point, he said to himself as he bobbed his head to the latest track by Landover's own Gunnaz & Bosses Entertainment. His cell phone began to vibrate. He looked down at the flashing screen, and noticing it was a private number, he hit ignore and dropped his J in the ashtray and stepped out. He hit his alarm and headed towards the entrance of the club. As he approached, party goers greeted him and dapped him. Most were genuine; others were just thirsty to get in fast.

"Sup, Boss man," Monty, his head of security, greeted as he lifted the velvet rope, so Ali could enter the club.

"Ain't shit but this money, Moe," Ali replied with a grin as he walked in, admiring the scenery.

Ali had 32 girls who worked for him and like Baskin Robins, they came in assorted flavors. Ten worked his escort service, ten worked Club Spread, and the remaining two were overseers while Ali wasn't around. He had come a long way from that petty pussy pusha he used to be as a youngster to the thirty-one-year-old, grown man entrepreneur he was today. Ali coined in on the quote, "Use what you got to get what you want", and with his ladies' man charisma, he came up. Ali was raised by a womanizer therefore he learned what he saw and put his gift of gab and dick game to work. Ali could talk a nun out her panties and life savings in a church. Yeah, he was smooth like that. As a teenager, he used to pimp his girlfriends out to the older neighborhood cats.

Now as an adult, here he was living the life. He had a thorough woman at home, Charli, who he actually loved. With living his life and with his reputation, it seemed like he'd never get right, but he'd never let anyone else have her either. He was surrounded by endless pussy at his disposal, money flowing thru his hands like the dams broke, and loyal niggas around him like Kazi and AK signed on as silent partners to Club Spread, doubling their profits as well.

***

Cherry spotted Ali as soon as he walked in. She was eyeing him like a predator eyes their prey. She watched him walk toward the DJ booth and engage in conversation with DJ Bam.

Ali chopped it up with DJ Bam for a second before he began to watch Fever who was now on-stage dancing to "Bait" by Wale. Fever had all eyes on her as she got on her hands and knees and began to make her ass clap to the rhythm of the song, and as she did splits and flips, the tips were flowing. "Damn mama you did dat...," a pretty young woman said as she approached the stage and rained a stack on Fever as she spread he legs and exposed her thick, cleanly shaven pussy lips.

"Mmmmmmm, welcome to Club Spread...," Fever said with a seductive grin, licking her lips.

"Work, Work, Work, Work!" DJ Bam said over the mic with a smile as he watched guys and girls alike walk over to tip the sexy Miss Fever.

Cherry saw her moment to move in while it seemed as if Ali was distracted.

"What's good, Daddy?" Cherry greeted Ali seductively, breaking Ali's daze by hugging him from behind. Ali turned to see Cherry, one of his new dancers standing there with a seductive grin and a mischievous look in her eyes, sucking the hell out of a watermelon Blow Pop.

"Mmm. Hey Miss Lady," he said as he hugged her back.

"I know you are a busy guy, but can I talk to you for a minute in private?" she asked as she raped him with her eyes.

"Yea, sure no problem," Ali replied as he led the way to his office. Cherry followed close behind.

  The tiny, baby doll nighty she wore left nothing to the imagination. Guys were pulling her arm asking for a VIP dance as she followed Ali. She smiled kindly and continued walking. She was on a mission. Ali walked in and had a seat behind his desk, giving Cherry his undivided attention.

"So, what is on your mind, Miss Cherry?" he asked as he leaned back in his chair.

An Uneasy Truth 2

"I need some of the action," she said, wasting no time getting to the point as she caressed his chest.

"What action would that be?" he asked, with a perplexed look on his face.

Cherry laughed at Ali as if he didn't catch the drift, so she dropped her blow pop in a glass that sat on his desk and unzipped his jeans, reached inside, and began stroking his thick, 9-and-a half-inch tool.

"This action," she said with a seductive smile.

"Dats too much for you, lil mama," Ali said in her ear.

She became moist almost instantly. She didn't bother saying another word. She slid down between his legs on her knees and placed his now hard tool into her wet, inviting mouth. She worked up her saliva sucking on the tip until she worked him deep into her throat. She went to work like she invented head slobbering, bobbing up and down his shaft as she exercised her throat muscles around his throbbing wood. "Damn, bitch. What the fuck?" Ali said as he gripped the back of her head. He could feel his nut brewing. Cherry abruptly stopped sucking and stood up. Ali was in complete bliss until she stopped.

"Oh, nahhh mu'fucka. I ain't done wit' you," she said as she straddled Ali and worked his thickness into her tight wet cave.

"Shit...," Ali said as Cherry rode his thick wood.

"It's not too much. This mu... fucka... is just... right...," Cherry moaned as she began to pick up the pace. Ali matched her rhythm with counter thrusts, pushing himself deeper into her and causing her to moan in pure bliss. Her wet tightness and her soft moans were pushing him over the edge.

"Fuck," he moaned, feeling his nut about to shoot.

As if they were reading each other's minds, Cherry got up off his wood which was now covered in her juices, got on her knees, and deep throated him until every drop had disappeared down her throat. She got up and wiped the mixture of her saliva and baby batter from her mouth and then walked away toward the bathroom in his office. She stopped before she walked in and said, "I'm small but I handle mine." Then she walked in the bathroom, closed the door, and cleaned herself up. Ali sat in his chair, still drunk off an orgasmic high, laughing to himself and thinking "Good shit come in small packages."

Cherry was on the other side of the bathroom door sending a text.

"Are you seriously paying me 10 stacks for dis? Too easy. It's in motion. TTYL." Then she continued cleaning herself up, so she could hit the floor and get this paper.

Chapter 17

"So, what are you doing here, Star?" Supreme asked, nudging Charli out of her thoughts. Her smile instantly fell, and her face became serious as the question registered in her brain. She had gotten so caught up in the moment that the reality had slipped to the back of her mind.

"Let's get some wings and move upstairs," Charli said in an exhausted tone as she weaved around the question. Supreme looked at Truth for an answer.

"Drama and bullshit," Truth said as she got up to follow Charli upstairs to VIP.

"Mack, let me get some wings and fries sent upstairs please."

"You got it," Mack said as he went to place their order.

"Thanks man," Supreme said as he shook his head laughing to himself.

Once they were all seated comfortably, Truth and Charli began to fill him in on the chain of events from a few hours ago.

"Damn, Truth. You was right. Drama and bullshit!" he laughed.

"I'm glad you find this bullshit entertaining," Truth said with a slight attitude as she looked down at her blinking cell phone. She picked it up and saw she had a text message. Thinking it was Leo finally returning her text, she hurried to open it. It read:

I want to see you. Meet me at the spot in Largo in about 40 min. –Sincere

Supreme and Charli were enjoying their wings while cracking jokes and laughing at the Unks at the bar like old times.

"Dats your uncle man. Go get him...," Supreme laughed, pointing out a fiend who had started to nod off in the corner. He had learned so far, they thought he would hit the floor. Just as it was

looking like he was floor bound, he sat straight up and start drinking his Heineken. All three of them erupted in laughter. Charli laughed so hard she had tears forming in her eyes.

"Boy, whatever," she said as she wiped the tears of laughter from her cheek.

Truth cracked up with them as she read the text from Sincere again for the fourth time, debating within herself what her next move would be. After about ten minutes of debating she decided she would meet him.

"Cha, you mind dropping me off in Largo?" Truth leaned over and whispered in Charli's ear.

Charli looked into Truth's pleading eyes and then turned to Supreme and asked, "You mind walking a lady to her vehicle?"

An Uneasy Truth 2

"Yeah. You know creeps be lurking at night on Benning Road," Truth said jokingly but was dead serious.

"Oh, y'all ready to bounce?" Supreme asked trying not to sound disappointed that he and Charli's reunion was cut short.

"Yeah, got some moves to make. Got to get some answers you know? Plus, got to make sure my little baby gets home safe," she replied with a smile, referring to Truth.

"Oh okay, drop your contact info in my device before we split," Supreme said, handing her his cell phone. Charli smiled as she did what he asked and then stood to leave. Supreme walked them out to the car. Truth climbed in the passenger seat and decided to try Leo again.

"Still no answer?" Charli asked, seeing the disappointed look her face as she got in and started the car and pulled into Benning Road traffic.

"Nahh, it's cool though. Just take me to the spot," Truth said with a slur in her speech.

Charli shook her head at her cousin's passive attitude towards the situation.

"Ay, cuz. You do realize somebody came for your head tonight in your home, correct?" Charli asked with a bit of aggravation in her voice. "And why the fuck was you drinking like that anyway? Bitch, you pregnant!" Charli continued, alternating her eyes between Truth and the road as she spoke.

"Damnit Cha! I got bitches coming for me on some death shit and I don't fucking know why. The nigga I'm in love is with treating me like shit on the bottom of his shoe like I don't fucking exist. There's a nigga that gives me all of that and more, but he is not mine and on top of all of that, there's a fucking baby in my belly. SHIT! I just want to enjoy this little buzz, fuck this nigga tonight, and regroup in the morning. So, dig this. If you about to get all mama militant and start coming down on me making me feel worse than I already do, then let me out. I'll walk," Truth replied with venom in her voice and a cold, drunken stare on Charli.

"Nahh, fam. I'ma make sure you get there safe." Charli was heated but she understood her frustration and let it roll off her back as they rode the rest of the way in silence. Charli pulled up at the spot and noticed Sincere's Chevy Suburban parked in front of the building.

"Cuz I love you. Text me in the a.m., okay?" Charli said, breaking the silence.

"I love you more...," Truth replied as she leaned over to hug her favorite cousin.

"Just text me in the a.m., ok?" Charli said as she wiped the single tear that trailed from Truth's eye.

Truth nodded, agreeing to text her before getting out to go inside the building. She was more confused now than when the night began and Charli as well. Just as Charli pulled off and headed home, her cell began to vibrate indicating she had a text:

"Get home safe Star." – Supreme

An Uneasy Truth 2

As she read it, a smile instantly spread across her face.

*****

Kima paced the waiting room anxiously for what seemed like hours waiting for the doctor to come out and give her news on Kasey.

"Excuse me Kima." Lisa, the nurse she encountered earlier walked up and gently touched her shoulder.

"Yes."

"The doctor would like to speak with you," Lisa said as she led the way to where the doctor was waiting. Kima followed Lisa down the hall feeling as if the air in her lungs was decreasing with every step she took closer to the doctor.

"Good evening, Ms……..?" the doctor inquired, extending his hand to Kima.

"Ms. Chase," she replied, shaking his hand.

"You are family, correct?" Dr. Greene asked, looking over Kasey's chart.

"Yes. She's my sister. How is she?" Kima lied with her voice full of genuine concern.

"Ok, calm down. Let's have a seat," he instructed as he pulled up a chair for Kima, seeing she was a bit shook.

"Well, Ms. Chase. Your sister is very lucky. We were able to stop the bleeding, remove the bullet, and save her life; however, she lost the baby."

"Oh, my God. What baby?" Kima asked in total shock.

"Ms. Bailey was approximately twelve weeks pregnant. We have her sedated for now and she'll be staying for observation, but we expect her to make a smooth recovery," Dr. Greene said as he stood to leave.

"Oh wow. Thank you, doc. May I see her?" Kima asked as she stood filled with guilt.

"Sure. But make it kind of speedy because visiting hours are over, and she'll need her rest to recuperate. Oh and Ms. Chase, please leave a contact number with the nurse for emergency purposes please," he replied as he showed Kima to Kasey's room and then disappeared through the double doors.

An Uneasy Truth 2

Chapter 18

Kima stood at the door looking at all the monitors, tubes and IV's attached to her friend. She slowly walked to her bedside and placed her hand on Kasey's hand. Instantly, tears flooded her face. She felt terrible.

"I'm so sorry, Kasey," Kima said as she took a seat in the chair next to Kasey's bed. "This is all fucked up man. Not only did I accidentally shoot my friend, but I'm responsible for the loss of her unborn child as well. I told her that shit was a bad idea. I fuckin' told her, but no she had to have Leo," Kima thought to herself as tear after tear fell from her eyes.

"I love you, Kase. Keep fighting. I'll be back tomorrow," Kima whispered to Kasey before she kissed her friend's cheek and left.

Kima got into her truck and broke down. After her vision was finally clear, she started her truck and pressed play on her system. "A Change Is Gonna Come" by Sam Cooke began to play as she got lost in her thoughts during her drive home. Kima was flooded with emotions: regret, sympathy, and anger. She regretted entertaining Kasey's emotional actions leading to the accidental shooting. She felt sympathy for her friend's loss because she knew the feeling of losing a child. She had just experienced that very same pain a few months back. While she was leaving Forestville Mall, three girls walked up on her demanding her new Jordan's and her Helly Hansen jacket.

Kima wasn't rocking like nothing so she punched the biggest of the three bitches and got her down on the ground. While they were fighting on the ground, Kima was getting out on her big ass. She had one hand wrapped in the girl's long braids and the other punched her over and over again until lumps formed on her head.

"Fuck you, bitch!" Kima said. With every punch she threw, she grew even more pissed.

"Lacey!" Tasha called out for her sister.

She was getting her ass kicked and she didn't intend on Kima being this serious or strong. Kima's 5'5", 145 lbs. frame was not letting Tasha's 5'11", 185 lbs. ass go. She held her tight in a leg lock, yo-yo'ing her ass with the blows of a man, stunning Tasha so much she balled up into a fetal potion. Seeing their sister getting fucked up enraged Lacey and Kelly. They started to stomp and punch Kima while she banged Tasha on the ground. Kima on the other hand didn't give a fuck. She kept punching and kicking, digging her nails into Tasha's face and eyes. She figured fuck it. Since they were going to jump her, she was going to make sure Tasha paid until somebody broke it up.

Lacey was determined to get Kima to off of Tasha. She could see she wasn't really fighting back so she began to stomp Kima in the head with her timberland cover foot.

An Uneasy Truth 2

After a few stomps and kicks Kima blacked out and woke up in the emergency room with a concussion, a few broken ribs, and the death of a baby she didn't know she was pregnant with; her and King's unborn child. As these thoughts ran through her mind, they fueled her anger toward Leo. Had he been a man about things and not lead Kasey on, none of the events of tonight would have even taken place.

"I'ma make you pay, Mister Leo," she said aloud as she headed to any spot Leo might be. First stop was Ali's place with anger in her heart and vengeance on her mind.

Cherry gave herself the once over before walking out of the bathroom.

"Aight, Daddy. I'll see you down stairs," she said as she sashayed past Ali toward the door who was now pouring himself a shot of Black Henny. He pulled the watermelon blow pop out his glass and smiled then handed it back to her.

'Aight, lil one," Ali laughed, smacking Cherry on the ass.

Damn shawty bad, Ali thought to himself as he took a seat. He turned on the 50-inch flat screen that hung on his office wall and tuned in to his security channel that displayed twelve live surveillance views of Club Spread. He sat in his office about fifteen minutes drinking on Black Henny, observing the party goers until he saw his niggas AK and Kazi arrive.

Cherry walked down the steps and out onto the now crowded floor. It was packed. All Cherry saw were dollar signs. Cherry was about 5 feet tall, pretty face, small waist, round ass, thick thighs, and a full C cup. Her build reminded some of Pinky, the porn star. Cherry was bad, and she knew it. Her light skin was covered in tattoos. She wore her hair in an asymmetric cut, similar to the super star Rihanna with fire red ends. It accentuated her hazel brown, almond-shaped eyes. Cherry pulled the attention of guys and girls as she walked through the club and out of nowhere, SMACK! She was damn near knocked on her ass, but she was quickly snatched back up before she could hit the ground.

"Damn dude," Cherry said with much attitude while regaining her balance. She looked up to see who was in a rush and damn near knocked her down. Her eyes fell on the sexiest chocolate man she had ever seen. She forgot all about almost being knocked on her ass.

"Oh shit. My bad. Excuse me, Redd," Roc said, apologetically placing a twenty-dollar bill in the garter that was wrapped snug around her thigh. He then continued in the direction of the stage.

Kazi's smooth, deep voice boomed over the speakers as he got Cypher Night started, breaking Cherry out of the sexually explicit thoughts she was now having about Roc.

"Welcome to Club Spread's Cypher Night. I'm one of your hosts, Kazi," Kazi began. The crowd cheered, showing him lots of love.

"We going to get things kicked off. For those of you who don't know, we have five simple rules:

1. Show love. It takes a lot to grace the stage.

2. No rapping and rolling. That's respect.

An Uneasy Truth 2

3. Tip your entertainment. These ladies are cutting up in here."

He laughed as he continued.

"4. Cut the beef. We are all here for the love of music. FIGHTING IS PROHIBITED!!

And last but not least, 5. Bring it! There are three hours of free studio time and a video on the line.

With that being said, I'm turning the mic over to my bro, AK," Kazi said as he passed AK the mic and he announced the first performers.

***

"Hey, mama. Your set is on stage three, okay?" Fever said after gently tapping Cherry on the shoulder.

"Okay, cool. Thanks, Fever," Cherry replied and then made her way toward stage three.

She stepped up onto the platform and admired her reflection in the three mirrors on the wall. She slowly swung around the pole with one hand. Her mind was on money and the mysterious chocolate guy as she began to pop her plump, round ass to the local artist who was performing on the main stage until a set of sexy twins walked up and sat at her stage in the corner amd started tipping her.

"What's good, brova?" AK said, walking up and giving Ali dap.

"Ain't shit, my nigga. Enjoying these new cats y'all brought out tonight," Ali said as he bobbed his head to the music.

"Yea, man. These lil dudes something serious. But ay, word on the street is Leo been fucking wit dat crazy bitch dat use shake her ass up in here. You heard from him?" AK asked.

"Man, that bitch is ill. She spazzed out because he broke the shit off. Crazy bitch flattened all four of his tires and rubbed shitty baby diapers all over his car," Ali laughed as he continued, "I told that mu'fucka she was wacked out. I fired her dumb ass for causing all that bullshit in front of my establishment while she was on the clock," Ali said shaking his head at the situation.

Leo was Ali's first cousin. Drop dead sexy, but seemed to pick the craziest females to deal with. The only good thing going for him was his persistent hustle ethic and Truth. She was something out of the ordinary-strong, beautiful, smart, and fly. Although Leo had his share of craziness, he got money by any means necessary. As an hour went by, different artist performed while some dancers went around to meet and greet club goers and others headed to VIP to show guests a good time. Ali couldn't help the uneasiness he was feeling, so he kept his eyes on his surroundings.

He had 12 security guards in attendance and on full alert-four at the door, four within the crowd, two on the VIP floor, and two at the back door as well as his twelve security cameras throughout the club.   Yet he still figured he would rather be safe than sorry since the only eyes one can trust are their own. He shook it off as maybe he was

An Uneasy Truth 2

just a little tipsy. Ali tapped AK and Kazi and signaled them to follow him to his office. He stopped by the DJ booth and handed him the artist line-up to announce and then the three continued to his office. Once in the office, they all grabbed a drink from the bar. Ali took a seat behind his desk, AK sat on the recliner near the bar, and Kazi sat on the loveseat with one of his long legs propped up.

"So, what's good my niggas?" Kazi asked, looking from Ali to AK.

"Well, my niggas' sales are looking excellent, customers are beyond satisfied, and beef is at an all-time low," AK replied in a cool and collected tone as he reclined in his chair and lit his Newport.

"That's what's up. And we doing good here at Club Spread along with S.P.P. (Street Pussy Profit, what he called his escort service). By the end of the year, we are going to be able to expand out west," Ali said rubbing his hands together, smiling and thinking of the come up.

"Yea, I'm with that. The studio is doing serious numbers. We booked up for another two months," Kazi said as he took a gulp of his drink. "We had a small situation a couple days ago; nothing serious. Some Looney ass bitch Leo be dealing with was in the lobby wrecking shit. I mean like straight fucking up the lobby all because he wouldn't come out and talk to her and when he finally did well y'all know the rest." Kazi scrunched his face up in disgust and took another gulp of his drink.

"See, that bullshit is bad for business," AK said, shaking his head at the foolery he had heard tonight involving Kasey.

"Yea, that's a problem that needs to be dealt wit ASAP. I'm bout to hit this nigga now because Kasey is a problem," Ali said sternly as he pulled out his cell to call Leo.

Chapter 19

Truth tapped lightly on the door. Within seconds, she could hear Sincere walking toward it. Her heart fluttered as the door opened. She stepped inside, fell into his arms, and began to cry. The alcohol was clearly taking over her emotions.

"What's wrong, Ma?" Sincere asked with concern as he ushered her to the leather sectional in his living room.

Sincere's spot was a small, comfy apartment he kept low-key. Its decorations were warm, neutral colors. It didn't look like a guy decorated it, but Sincere did it himself. He had taste. The tears just continued to flow as Truth buried her face in his tatted, muscular chest. Sincere just held her as she cried, unsure of the reason. He didn't like seeing her hurt because he had grown feelings for her since they started kicking it a year ago. Sincere and Truth met a year prior while Leo was locked up in DC jail on a distribution charge. Truth and Charli went to one of their friend's bachelorette party at a hotel in Greenbelt.

It all started that night...

"Damn, Cha. You ain't say Nita was having girl strippers," Truth said, rolling her eyes.

"Well, you didn't ask. Plus, what do you expect? She is a lesbian," Charli laughed as she took a seat to get a good view when then show began.

Charli wasn't a lesbian, but exotic dancers intrigued her and turned her on. Plus, she was very secure in herself; enough so that giving the next female their props was second nature.

"Well, I'ma go hit this J in the car. By the time I get back, their set will be over, right?" Truth asked as she grabbed her purse in route to the door.

"See you in a minute, T," Charli said, laughing at Truth as she hurried out the door as the first dancer's music came on.

Truth rushed out the door so fast that she wasn't looking where she was going and ran into Sincere, who was standing outside smoking his Black and Mild. Truth had knocked it out of his hand as she ran out of the door and ran into him. They both bent down to pick it up at the same time and bumped heads.

"Shit!" Truth laughed as she rubbed the sore spot on her forehead then handed him his Black and Mild.

"Where you in a rush to?" Sincere laughed, rubbing the bump now forming on his head after colliding with Truth's head.

"To hit this J. Care to join me? It's the least I can do since I lumped you up," Truth said as she reached over and rubbed the knot on his head.

"Hell, why not?" he laughed as they began to walk toward the parking lot.

"We can sit in my truck if you want. I don't bite," Sincere suggested with a sexy grin.

She nodded her approval with a smile and followed him to his truck. I wonder what he is doing here or who he is doing here rather, she thought to herself.

***

Sincere hit the locks and climbed in on the driver's side. Truth was a little hesitant at first because she didn't know him, but his aura screamed security, so she climbed in the passenger's side and lit the J of Maui Waui that she had pre-rolled out of her purse.

"So, who are you?" Truth asked as she took a long pull of the blunt.

"I'm Sincere. And you are?" He laughed at Truth as she started to choke a little and pass him the blunt.

"I'm Truth. So, you came here with your girl or something?" she asked as she turned to face him a little more.

"Nah. I'm security for two dancers who are here doing a bachelorette party inside. And I don't have a lady. If I did, we wouldn't be having this convo," he replied with a sly smirk.

An Uneasy Truth 2

"Oh, really? Well, that's good to know. I wouldn't want my man sitting in a car with a random chick at a hotel blazing either," Truth replied honestly she retrieved the blunt.

"Yea, it's all about respect," he said sincerely as he turned on his system. "All We Do" by Young Jeezy played thru the speakers.

"Ooooooo, this my shit," Truth said as she started to rap along with Jeezy.

Sincere just bobbed his head to the beat and admired Truth's beauty. Damn she is gorgeous, he thought to himself. They laughed, joked, and got to know each for a couple of hours well after the blunt was gone. Before they knew it, both their cells were getting text messages asking where they were. Truth's text was from Charli and Sincere's from Kasey and Cream, two of Ali's dancers from Club Spread.

"Damn, I guess we'd better get back," Truth said as she began to climb out of the truck.

"Yeah, I got to drop these girls off," Sincere agreed as he followed alongside Truth.

"Let me see your phone," Truth said as they headed inside the entrance of the hotel. She locked her number in his phone and they agreed to keep in touch before parting ways.

A year later, here they were only difference was he was now he had a woman in his life who he cared for but he loved Truth...

"Ma, are you going to tell me what's wrong?" Sincere asked in a comforting tone, lifting Truth's chin so he could look into her eyes. Truth's sad eyes met his.

"Somebody wants me dead," she said before jumping up running to the bathroom and hurling up her guts.

Sincere sat on the sofa dumbfounded as he waited for Truth to come back. After about fifteen minutes went by and she didn't return, he went to go check on her only to find her in her bra and panties passed out, curled up in fetal position. He just climbed in bed and held her as she slept. Inside he was angry and wanted to know what was going on but decided to let her sleep off the alcohol and get answers in the morning.

***

Charli rode home listening to "For the Good Times" by Al Green as thoughts of Supreme ran through her head. She pulled into her parking lot and was glad to see a parking spot in front of her building available. She parked and read Supreme's text again. Damn, I've missed him, she thought to herself as she replied to his text: Made it home safe. Thanks. Goodnight. XOXO. After she hit send, she looked around the parking lot through her tints. She was always aware of her surroundings, but she had the feeling she was being watched. She tucked her pistol in the small of her back pulled down her t-shirt before getting out. She then made her way to her building.

Once she made it in her apartment, safe and sound, she stripped down to her boy shorts, tank top, and socks. She headed straight to her bed, dropping items on her way.

An Uneasy Truth 2

Charli laying there in bed in complete darkness with so many thoughts running thru her head. She tried relaxing her mind and finally dozed off. Just as she drifted into a good sleep, someone started banging on the front door, startling her right back out of it. She jumped out of her bed, quickly snatched up her robe, and threw it on. She stormed to the door, mad as shit that somebody had awakened her from her drunken slumber. As she got closer to the door, the banging became persistent. Charli didn't even look through the peep hole to see who it was. She just unlocked it and snatched the door open.

"Mu'fucka do you know...," she began yelling but got cut off.

"Didn't you get my fucking text, young?" AK asked, pushing past Charli.

"Khalil King, are you fucking serious right now? You come banging on my fucking door like the police because I didn't reply to your fucking text?!?! Get the fuck, young!" Charli yelled in AK's face with a mean mug.

She then walked into her kitchen to get a bottle of water since she was still feeling her drinks from earlier. AK walked up behind her, wrapped his arms her waist, and began planting sensual kisses on the back of her neck, dismissing her anger about being awakened and her attitude.

"Go 'head Khalil. I told you I'm not with this," Charli said as she pulled out of his embrace.

AK had a thing for Charli since the day they met seven years ago when she and Ali were just getting serious but that didn't stop AK from pursuing her on the low. Although AK would come with tangible evidence, Charli wasn't the tit for tat type of female. She declined AK's advances every time. AK was the homie and they were close and all, but she wasn't a homie hopper. In her eyes, the sooner he realized that the sooner his feelings would stop getting hurt.

"Why you keep calling me that shit, man?" AK asked as he took a seat at the dinning table and rolled a J of granddaddy purp.

"Because mu'fucka. It's your name. I don't know "AK". I know Khalil King," she said as she smacked him upside his head while slightly stumbling to the couch.

"Mannnn... anyway where you been?" he asked as he licked the leaf to seal the blunt.

"Ha... ha... Bring dat J. I got a story to tell," She imitated Biggie as she propped her feet up and patted the seat next to her, signaling him to sit next to her.

"Well, some chick came for Truth's head tonight," Charli said as she took another sip of her water.

"What? Nah. Not Truth. She a good girl.," AK said as he shook his head in disbelief.

AK was in total shock. He couldn't see Truth pushing nobody to want to kill her. Kick her ass maybe because of jealousy or shit talking, but not snatch her life.

"Mann... it's something else behind that shit. Don't you go playing stiletto high private eye trying to get answers cause the last thing I want to see is you or Truth hurt. You tell Ali yet?" he asked as he hit the blunt and passed it to Charli.

An Uneasy Truth 2

"Nah, I haven't talked to Ali since earlier, but I've been wrecking my brain trying to figure out why and most importantly, who would want to violate. And you know better. That's my blood. I'm not rocking. I'ma handle whoever, straight like that," she replied as she took two more short pulls from the blunt and passed it back to AK.

Charli was still buzzed from a couple hours ago and the J was boosting her buzz. She could feel the room spinning as she laid her head against the back of the sofa. AK looked at her and tried to shake wanting her, but he couldn't help it. She was beautiful, inside and out. It was wrong because she was his right-hand man's woman, but it felt right saving her from heartache with Ali. Ali was his right-hand man, but he was all wrong for Charli in his eyes. I just want to love her. I'm not perfect, but I can be for her, Khalil thought to himself as he sat in a daze, staring at Charli.

Chapter 20

"What you thinking about?" Charli asked with a puzzled look and her head still spinning. She knew she needed to lie down soon.

"It ain't shit you don't know already," Khalil said as he leaned in close and started kissing on her neck. He wanted her bad. He just prayed she would say yes.

"I'm on a money making' mission…," 2 Chainz' lyrics blared from her cell phone, letting her know her niece was calling.

Whew… saved by the bell, Charli thought to herself as she got up quickly to go to the bedroom to answer her cell phone.

"Hello."

"Hey auntie."

"Hey, Hun. What's up? What time is it?" Charli asked.

An Uneasy Truth 2

"It's almost two. I'm sorry if I woke you up, but I just needed somebody to talk to on my way home," Kandy said with a slur.

"It's okay. You sound like you had a few. I'll stay on the phone with you until you get home. You know I don't like you riding solo and buzzed late at night," Charli said.

"Yeah. I know, auntie. I'm Jy wasted. I went to perform with a few of the homies tonight at uncle club and had one too many," Kandy laughed, "but I'm almost home though. In 'bout five more minutes," she said as she approached the stop light a block away from her apartment complex.

Charli lay stretched across her bed in the dark with her eyes closed, listening to Kandy tell her about her night. Khalil used her call as the distraction he needed. He walked in and placed himself between Charli's legs, kneeled down, pulled her boy shorts to the side, and parted her thick lips with his tongue in search of her pearl. AK's actions caught Charli totally off guard. She wanted him to stop because she knew it was wrong, but it was feeling so good. Kandy continued to talk in her ear, but the things AK was doing to her left her ears deaf and her mouth mute. AK licked her throbbing pearl and slowly her juices began to cover his lips. She was in complete bliss as he gradually sped up when he felt her palm his head.

"Auntie!! Did you hear me? I'm home!!!" Kandy yelled, snapping Charli out of her orgasmic paralysis.

"Oh, shit. Okay," she said before hanging up.

Khalil on the other hand wasn't done. He had swiftly removed her boy shorts and proceeded going to work sticking his tongue deep into her wetness. His thick, warm, wet tongue was doing magic tricks on her box and she was lost in the satisfaction She couldn't control her orgasms. She gripped the back of his head when he began licking her from her clit to her ass and then gently taking her throbbing clit in his mouth and sucking it while fingering her.

"Mmmmmmm, Mmmmmmm, yessss...," Charli moaned.

He drove Charli up the wall as he pushed two of his fingers inside her wetness. So much so that she couldn't contain herself and she began to rock back and forth on his face, eventually squirting on his chin and fingers.

"Fuck!" she yelled as she lay there, trying to regain her breath and regular heartbeat. She felt like shit deep down inside, but it sure felt good.

Khalil stood up, sucked Charli's juices off his finger, then wiped his chin with his hand and turned to leave.

"Oh. And that's what I was thinking 'bout. Thanks for coming baby," Khalil said and then left. Charli just laid there lost in her thoughts. What the fuck just happened?

She could barely move to lock her front door her energy was so drained. But as she made her way to do so everything AK had just did to her replayed in her mind causing her knees felt like they wanted to buckle on her. She made her way back to her king-sized bed and drifted off to sleep peaceful and pleased.

An Uneasy Truth 2

Daylight crept through the blinds as bacon invaded Truths nostrils causing her to become nauseous she jumped up and ran to the bathroom almost knocking the tray of food Sincere was holding in his hand. "Damn T!" he yelled as he sat the tray on the nightstand and trailed her to the bathroom. "I'm sorry baby." Truth managed to say as she released what felt like her soul in the toilet. "You ok? This not like you." Sincere asked as he wet a washrag in cold and laid it on the back of Truths neck. She didn't wanna tell him this way without truly knowing who's baby she was carrying or if she even wanted to keep it.

She got up brushed her teeth and washed her face as Sincere went back and began to eat the Belgium waffles and bacon he had prepared for Truth and himself. Truth gathered her thoughts and joined him in bed. "You wanna tell me what's going on with you?" Sincere inquired calmly as he cut into his waffles.

"Sin, I'm pregnant." Truth replied sounding defeated.

"You were clearly drunk when you came to me, so you knew this before the drinks right?" Sincere asked as he sat his plate on the nightstand suddenly losing his appetite.

"Yes." Truth replied feeling more like shit than she did having to tell him it may not even be his. He wasn't a dumb guy he knew the possibilities of it being his were half but possibilities none the less. He didn't even bother carrying on the conversation and decided to just enjoy her presence and worry about the situation later.

"Where you going?" Truth asked seeing him throw on a pair of sweatpants and a t shirt.

"I'mma go for a run, you eat that breakfast and rest. I'll be back shortly. He said as he leaned in and kissed her soft plump lips before leaving.

"Oh, and Truth." Sincere stopped in his steps before walking out the room.

"Yes Sin?"

"This conversation will continue at a later time." And he walked out the door closing it behind him.

Truth ate the bacon and curled up holding Sincere's pillow surprisingly the bacon stayed down, she drifted off to sleep with peaceful thoughts.

"Hey you." Ali said gently waking Charli from her hard sleep with a Ihop bag in his hand. "Heyy." Charli said groggily as her eyes adjusted to the Sunlight that was blinding her drunken eyes.

"Damn you ok? Look like you had a long night." Ali asked as he began to remove the food from the bag.

An Uneasy Truth 2

"Bitches tried to kill Truth last night." Charli said as she got out of bed and slid into her slippers.

"The fuck you mean? And why the bed wet right here" Ali asked in shock as he noticed the wet spot at the end if the bed.

"Yea that's what I said so you already know it's war. And umm I dropped a glass trying to climb on that bed last night. " She said from the open bathroom door as she sat on the toilet. She was so drained she forgot to change the damn comforter.

"From the toilet gangster?" Ali tried to make light of the situation, in his mind he already knew how she went about her blood.

"Oh, you got jokes I see." Charli laughed as she smooched Ali's head as she climbed on the bed, she retrieved her food from the bag and dug into her sausage, pancakes, hash browns and scrambled eggs with cheese. Glad he skipped the topic if that wet spot.

"I see you don't, but check this out stay the fuck out of that shit. Blood or not Truth is grown. I don't care what we go through I couldn't imagine losing you behind somebody else bullshit." Ali said stern yet sincere.

"I hear what you saying but..." Charli began but was interrupted by the vibrating of her cellphone on the nightstand. She sat her food aside picked up her cellphone seeing it was Truth.

"Hello." Charli answered

"Hey you." Truth said in a somber tone.

"What's wrong?" Charli asked she kind of had an idea her mood circled around last night's events.

"What's not wrong at this moment. All I wanna do is model Cha, but I'm knocked up and a set of bitches clearly want me dead. Shit the way things looking I'mma probably be dead before I even have this baby or be a model." Truth said sounding defeated as she sat on the side of Sincere's bed shaking her head.

"Everything will be fine cuz trust me." Charli said before sitting her food down and finding something to wear for the day.

"I hear you. I'm about to get up and get ready I feel like shit, but I don't think Sin really wants me around right now." Truth said as she gathered a pair of sweatpants and a t-shirt she had in Sincere's closet.

"I'm already getting dressed be there in thirty-five minutes be outside please." Charli said as she brushed her teeth.

"Okay see you in a few." Truth said before hanging up. She wasn't sure where Sincere had went for his jog and she hoped she would be gone before he got back because she really didn't wanna discuss it and felt crazy for mentioning it knowing her circumstances.

Thirty-five minutes passed and true to her word Charli was sitting outside Truth ran out and jumped in the car.

"I guess we're going to check on the house." She said as she slumped down in the passenger seat. Charli just nodded and drove to Truth's house she knew her cousin had a lot on her mind, so she just turned up the music and they rode in silence.

"Oh, look who decides to show up." Truth said as she and Charli got out of the car and walked toward the house.

"Oh shit." Charli mumbled to herself as Truth took off and slammed her fist into Leo's nose causing blood to squirt everywhere.

"you're crazy bitch!" Leo yelled as he covered his nose and moved around dodging more blows from Truth.

"Nahh mu'fucka you the crazy one come here like shit all good after bitches come here gunning for me!" Truth screamed at him.

"What?!" Leo yelled as he tried his best to stop the bleeding from his nose.

"Come on go inside." Charli said as she pulled Truth inside the house and Leo followed.

"I got somebody coming to fix the door, I don't know shit about what you talking about." Leo said as he held his head up and covered his nose with a dish towel.

"Well while you were gone doing whatever is it the fuck you do two bitches kicked the door in and was coming for my head one of the stupid bitches shot the other and they kicked it." Truth said pointing to the trail of dry blood from the living room to the front door.

Buzz.. Charli's cellphone vibrated indicating she had a text.

Isis: Hey cuz meet me at mommy's.

Charli: Ok

"Look I'm headed to Benning road, you riding?" Charli interrupted Truth and Leo arguing.

"I sure am." Truth said before leaving with Charli.

When they got to Nadine's she could see the stressed look in Truth's face.

"What's wrong baby?" Nadine asked as she sat next to Truth. Truth told her all about what she had been going

An Uneasy Truth 2

through with Leo and how she too had stepped out and was now pregnant and didn't know what man was the father. Nadine in return told her own story leaving the girl's in awe Isis had no clue of any of this so she sat with her mouth agape.

"We have to end this cycle now. Truth I can't tell you what to do just whatever you do make sure it's best for you." Nadine said lovingly. Charli sat analyzing her own situation now that Supreme was back it was bringing back old feelings. After their very much needed heart to heart with Nadine they headed to the Mall for some retail therapy Truth bought just enough clothes to stay with Sincere for the week or longer and had Charli drop her off when they were done.

SUPREME***

"I wiped down the tables Mack, I'm headed out back for a smoke break." I said as I walked toward the back to hang the rag and dump the water bucket I was using. As I walked out the back door my cellphone started to vibrate I pulled it out my pocket to see it was Cherry one of my little stripper homies I had working at Club Spread.

"Hello." I answered.

"What's up daddy? That Mark was a little too easy." She said referring to Ali.

"That's good, that's good. Come see me in the next hour for the next step." Supreme said before hanging up. He had a whole plan mapped out, he was determined to have Charli by any means necessary.

As he stood out back smoking his Newport he attempted to call Valerie once again when her phone went straight to voicemail he hung up and called Destiny.

"Hey lil sis, have you spoke to Valerie I been trying to catch up with her?" Supreme asked with concern in his voice. No matter what they went through he loved his sister.

"Not since she packed her stuff and dropped VJ off she said she needed a break." Destiny lied she knew exactly what happened to Valerie and felt no sadness about it.

"Oh, ok so you have VJ that's good, I'm going to swing by to see y'all at the end of the week." Supreme said

"Oh, ok that's cool, let me finish cooking I'll talk to you later love you bro." Destiny said before hanging up. She had just lied to her brother something she didn't do and though she loved both of her siblings protecting VJ was more important.

"Oh, ok love you too." Supreme said before hanging up he could sense something wasn't right but decided he would let things play out. Supreme tossed his cigarette and headed back inside the bar later meeting up with Cherry.

"Hey daddy." Cherry purred in his ear before taking a seat next to him on a booth.

"Wassup beautiful. Here put this in your purse." Supreme said as he slid her a thick envelope with five thousand dollars in it and a small baggie that contained what looked like two tiny Alka-Seltzer tablets.

"Okay I know what to do with the envelope, but what about the contents of the baggie?" Cherry asked with a confused look on her face she had been paid to do weird shit in her day.

"Drop 'em in the nigga drink and call me when you do. That's all job complete." Supreme replied with a grin as he sat back in his seat.

"Oh shit, yea this is the easiest job I've ever had." She said as she rose from the booth and kissed Supreme on the cheek before leaving just as quite as she came.

Supreme: "Hey beautiful."

Charli: "Hey you. What's up?"

Supreme: "You. Let's go to Friday's later."

Charli: "Sure, I'll meet you at your job before you get off."

Supreme: "Bet."

Supreme wasn't walking away without the girl this time and he was gonna make damn sure of that.

Later that night Cherry strutted into Club Spread on a mission and wasn't leaving until it was executed. The club was jumping, VIP was full, liquor was flowing, the DJ was doing his thing and the dancers were on point. "Oh, hell yeah its packed in here." Cherry thought to herself as she maneuvered through the crowded club to the dressing room.

"Heyy y'all." Cherry said to the other dancers in a happy tone as she entered the dressing room.

"Hey girl." They all spoke in random order.

An Uneasy Truth 2

"Umm Cherry can I talk to you in the back room." Mystique asked softly in Cherry's ear. Cherry had just stepped out of her clothes and slid into a short robe and followed Mystique to the lounge.

Mystique swiftly closed the door behind them and locked it. Before Cherry could get a word out she had pounced on her straddling her pinning her to the sofa that sat along the wall.

"I missed you, where you been?" Mystique said as she kissed up and down Cherry's neck and face grinding her pelvis against Cherry's lap.

"Damnn Mystique." Cherry moaned as Mystique trailed kisses down her belly and placed her warm tongue against Cherry's clit inhaling her scent drove Mystique crazy and she began to sloppily lick and suck on Cherry's clit. Cherry went wild grabbing the back of Mystique's head and grinding on her face until she reached her climax.

"I'm sorry I couldn't help myself." Mystique said as she stood and wiped her face and mouth.

"You're gonna make me fall in love with you." Cherry said before fixing her clothes and leaving the lounge. She and Mystique had been having these random sexual encounters for a few months ever since they did their first lesbian bachelor party together. Cherry nor Mystique could actually say they were lesbians because they loved dick but loved having sex with each other only.

Cherry took a quick rinse off and got dressed, stuck the baggie that contained the two little white tablets in her top and headed to the floor. She scanned the floor for Ali and when she spotted him he was near the elevator talking to the set of bad ass twins that were tipping her heavily a few nights prior one wearing black leggings that looked like they were painted on and a pink tight mid drift t-shirt and the other where red and black leggings with IMAJEAN COLLECTION down the side with a black tight matching mid drift. "Damn both them bitches bad." Cherry thought admiring the women.

She made her way closer and waited for Ali to be alone once he was she made her move.

"Hey handsome, you got something for me?" Cherry purred in his ear as she slid her tiny hand over his crotch.

"Well damn, that's one hell of a hello." Ali chuckled as he grabbed her tiny hand and led her to his office. Once they were inside he couldn't keep his hands off her and that's just how she wanted it she learned early In life once you got 'em by the dick they comply.

"Hold on hold on, can I have something to drink please sir?" she chuckled as she pulled his hands out her thong. She could feel his dick throbbing through his jeans "Got him by the dick." She thought to herself.

"Yeah sure, but you did just have your hands all over my dick like you was ready to go right now." Ali laughed as he poured them both a double shot of tequila.

"Here you go sweetheart. I'll be right back." Ali said handing her the shot he poured for her. He left his cellphone on the DJ station and didn't wanna miss this business call about expanding his club to Cali, thanks to Leo he had a hard to come by connect with an even harder to come by price.

"Timing couldn't be better." She said as she walked over to his shot and dropped the tablets in they dissolved quickly, and she took a seat on the loveseat in his office as she sent the text to Supreme letting him know they were dropped. Supreme sat in the rental outside the back door of the club waiting.

"Ok, where were we?" Ali said as he strolled back in his office.

"Umm you were taking your shot. And then bout to climb up in this pussy." She replied seductively as she spread her legs for him to see her now exposed cleanly shaved pussy.

"Fuck yea." Ali replied with a grin before taking his shot to the head. He began to walk over to Cherry but collapsed before making it to the loveseat.

"Shit!" Cherry said before dialing Supreme.

"Go back downstairs act normal, say nothing about him to anyone and again act normal lil' mama." Supreme whispered through the phone as he crept through the crowd and to the elevator. Fortunately for him back door security had the night off.

"Okay." Cherry said nervously before hanging up going downstairs and leaving. She knew she couldn't fake normal, so it was best to just disappear.

Supreme pushed a black laundry cart onto the elevator and went up once he was inside he stuffed Ali in a huge trash bag and wheeled him out the back of the club, tossed the bag in his trunk and pulled off into the night with not a soul knowing what was happening.

An Uneasy Truth 2

Supreme pulled into a dark alley and unloaded the trunk he carried the bag into the basement of a small house he tossed the bag on the floor as if it were trash, opened it up and tied an unconscious Ali to a metal chair that was cemented into the floor and left. As he pulled away from the house he called Charli to make sure they were still on before heading to his sister Destiny's apartment to chill with them and freshen up before his date with Charli.

"Damn who is that?" Supreme asked with a raised eyebrow referring to the picture Destiny and Isis took at Club Spread the night they went out.

"Oh, that's my girl Isis she's Mel's big sister." Destiny said with a smile she loved Isis to death she was the big sister she always wanted.

"Oh yea?" Supreme said with a smirk.

"Oh hell Nahh 'Preme. We not doing all that last time you tried to talk to one of Valerie friends we had to end up beating the shit outta the girl. I love Isis I won't allow that. Besides don't you got bitches?" Destiny said as she moved around her room.

"Nope not a one... not the one I want." Supreme said honestly.

"Well my brotha that ain't what you want." Destiny said meaning every word.

"I guess you right. I guess." Supreme said lightly punching Destiny in the arm and walking into the spare bedroom to get ready for his date with Charli. He loved his baby sister and respected her word. So, for now Isis was off limits but only for now.

An hour in a half later Supreme pulled into a parking spot at the bar and waited for Charli to pull up. Tap tap tap. He looked over and she was standing at his passenger door.

"You looking for me?" She asked with a smile as she climbed inside.

"Yeah I thought you were driving. You ready?" Supreme said as he started his car.

"Oh, I parked at mommy's and walked over through the alley." She laughed as she buckled her seatbelt indicating she was ready. Supreme pulled into traffic and drove to the T.G.I Fridays in greenbelt, they talked all the way there laughing and reminiscing about old times. As always there were motorcycles and drama all over the parking lot they laughed and bypassed it all and went inside.

An Uneasy Truth 2

After eating good and tossing back five margaritas a piece they were both feeling it.

"I'm ready to go." Charli said starting1 feeling her drinks.

"You got it." Supreme said before paying the bill.

"Where you wanna go Star?" Supreme asked looking between the road and Charli who had her seat leaned all the way back with one foot on the dash board.

"Where you wanna take me?" Charli replied seductively those margaritas were in full effect now.

"Say no more." Supreme said as he weaved through traffic listening to "Never had a friend" by 2pac.

They arrived at the Washington Suites in Alexandria, Virginia. They got out of the car Supreme assisted Charli seeing her wobbling a bit she sat on a plush nearby bench as he paid for the room. Once that was done they went up in the elevator kissing and touching all over each other all the way. A Caucasian woman stepped on as they were going up they paid her no mind as they continued to kiss and grope all over each other. "Get a room." She said with her nose turned up as she stepped off the elevator. Supreme nicely held up his key never breaking his kiss from Charli as the doors closed in the woman's face. They made it to their room and clothes flew everywhere as they snatched them off of each other 1and tossed them wherever they may land.

"I been waiting for this." Supreme said as he lifted Charli and pushed the beautiful table placement on the floor as he placed her on the dining table.

"Oooo shit. Me too." Charli said seductively as Supreme kissed and caressed her body. They made love all over that room for hours before Charli passed out on the bed.

"Hey you hungry?" Supreme asked as he gently kissed Charli's sleeping lips he had walked to Waffle house while she was sleeping and ordered her some breakfast her favorite bacon, fried potatoes and Belgium waffles with orange-pineapple juice.

"Mmmm that smells good." She said still groggy as she sat up in bed trying to focus.

"Got you some breakfast and you should get up we got a few moves to make." Supreme said as he kissed her lips and sat the tray of food in front of her.

"We?" Charli said as she took a bite of bacon.

An Uneasy Truth 2

"exactly so eat up I'm going to get ready. You got a bag in the closet." He said before getting up and heading into the bathroom. Charli sat the food on the bed once he left the room and opened the closet to see two hangers one had a flawless custom Jon Marc gown covered in a garment bag and it had to be custom because they specialize in plus size attire and the other was a cute all black one-piece sleeveless jumper with lipsticks, compacts, the capital and a few hand prints all over it the logo let her know it was from the Imajean collection she stepped back impressed, she loved what Supreme picked out and at this point couldn't wait to see what he had planned. She ate a little more of her breakfast and crept into the bathroom while Supreme was still showering and stepped inside.

"What you doing girl?" Supreme tried to ask but his words got caught in his throat as Charli deep throated his thick tool she went to work in that shower, something about Supreme made her forget all about Ali and she loved it.

After putting in a sexual workout they showered and got dressed, Supreme took Charli shopping and to the casino. He didn't have to work so he intended on spending his day with Charli.

"Hey Uncle Loco is having a function tonight, you trying to go with me?" Charli asked after reading the text from Shell.

"Hell yeah, Loco my man." Supreme replied with a bit of excitement, he met Loco while they were locked up and had been keeping in contact ever since.

"Okay Bet. So that's the move." She said as she sat back in her seat and looked out the window she wondered why Ali hadn't called her or blew up her texts as he usually does when she doesn't come home but the thought flew right out her mind as Supreme grabbed her hand and kissed it.

Charli didn't know it, but he had an entire weekend planned for her if she just went with the flow.

After the function at Nadine and Loco's apartment the Charli and Supreme went back to Washington suites for the remainder of the weekend. Days and nights went by with no word from Ali, Charli shrugged it off she was used to him disappearing for days she chose not to sit around and sulk about it though Supreme was keeping her mind and body occupied.

Boom Boom Boom Boom!! Someone banged on Charli's front door.

An Uneasy Truth 2

"Who the fuck is that?" Charli said to herself as she put the remote on the couch and went to get the door.

"The fuck is you banging on my mufuckin door like that for Leo!" Charli yelled, his cousin had been missing in action for over a month and he was determined to get answers.

"Where the fuck is Ali?" Leo said as he paced the living room.

"You tell me. I ain't seen that nigga in almost two months." Charli yelled back with her hand on her hip. "How dare this mu'fucka come in here questioning me about his dumb ass cousin." She thought to herself.

"Charli if I find out you got anything to do with my blood missing it's gonna..." Leo was saying before "Click click" a pistol cocked back, and he could feel the cold steel pressed against his temple.

"Gonna be what sir?" Supreme asked through clenched teeth.

"I think you should go Leo." Charli said with an eyebrow raised. As far as she was concerned she and Ali were through.

"Yea aight." Leo said as he walked out the door toward his car.

"There his ass go right there." Kasey said to herself as she sat in her car waiting for Leo to come back out of the building, she had been following him for the past two days and finally he was alone, and she could get at him. It was his fault her friend was fighting for her life in the hospital had he just been a man about what he wanted Kima wouldn't have lost her baby, got shot or would be in the hospital due to them going to murder Truth his girlfriend.

Leo walked slowly to his police tinted crown Victoria looking down texting as Kasey crept out the cut dressed in all black with a oversized black hoodie and mask with pistol in hand. Mahogany sat in the passenger seat playing with the radio station when she saw a glare out of her peripheral vision. As soon as Kasey sent the first shot Mahogany sent the last one hitting her in the center of her forehead. Leo had ducked behind a nearby car when the first shot rang off after the second he heard Mahogany yelled "Let's go!" He jumped in the car and they peeled out they could hear sirens in the distance when they looked at each other and released a sigh of relief.

An Uneasy Truth 2

"Thank god for you." Leo said as he looked over at his trigger happy big cousin as she tucked her pistol back inside her Darkside collection hobo bag.

"I love you too boy. Stop loafin' I don't know what that shit was about but you gotta get it together, bitches gunning for Truth now they gunning at you. Whatever you doing kill it and make a choice 'cause if you haven't noticed bitches is getting dead behind the D." she said referring to her having to shoot some female in the head back there.

"I will cuz, I'mma fix it." Leo said as he drove down I-95.

**Meanwhile in a basement in uptown D.C **

"Where the fuck am I?" Ali said aloud as his eye tried to adjust to the shinning light in his face. He struggled to move but was still tied to the chair.

"Oh good you're awake." Supreme said as he stepped out of the shadows.

"FUCK NAHH.." Ali said in disbelief. He couldn't believe Charli's old jump off had him in this situation.

"Oh fuck yess." Supreme replied with a grin as he pulled up a chair in front of Ali.

"What the fuck do you want?" Ali asked staring Supreme straight in the eyes.

"You see brother, its not about what I want because I have that. Supreme said referring to Charli. I'm taking what's due to her now." Supreme said cockily as he sat back in the chair.

"So you kidnapped your own brother for a bitch? I always knew she would be your downfall." Ali grinned.

"You have never been a brother to me we just share the same blood lets correct that. Anyway I doe time for the back in forth sign over all your businesses to Charli." Supreme replied nonchalantly. He didn't give two shits about Ali being his brother by his dad. "the mufucka ain't give two shits when he gave me to the state to get me put the picture to have Charli to himself." Supreme thought to himself.

"Nigga you might as well kill me now, I ain't leaving you and my bitch no happily ever after." Ali spat angrily. The truth was he told the narcs where they could find a drug transport and that transport being Supreme who was moving weight for Ali. Its was in his mind the only way to keep Supreme away from Charli and he took it.

An Uneasy Truth 2

"Bro honestly even if I let you go you wouldn't survive out there because you're a rat. Sign the papers." Supreme said as he untied Ali's right hand and handed him the documents. He knew Ali wouldn't and couldn't try anything with only one hand free. Nor could Ali handle Supreme in a one on one so all odds were against Ali in this situation. Ali signed the papers reluctantly and took his L. Supreme then stood back and cocked his .45 with the silencer and put two in the front of Ali's skull. He then left and went to the post office and mailed the documents to Charli with no return address and was off to work as if nothing happened.

Chapter 21

Isis

5 years later...

"Come on mommy." Sky said with joy as she grabbed my hands and pulled me to the center of the floor to dance with her. It was Sky's sweet sixteen and here I was big as a house dancing around without a care in the world. I love my daughter. She is my light, that little version of me I always have to check. I glanced over at the crowd and

An Uneasy Truth 2

everyone looks so happy, laughing, and dancing with smiles on their faces.

My sons and nephew—yeah yeah I said sons. I decided to adopt VJ after his mom disappeared without a trace. I always wonder what I would have really found out had we ever sat down and talked or if Mel didn't kill Vee would I had ever known him. VJ was over there trying to kick game to a couple of Sky's good girl friends like typical teen age boys. So, yea I have two and a half sons now. Troy and I are expecting; I love that man he is truly a dream come true I've never been happier with my family coming full circle and working full time at Royal Reign as executives designer. I looked over at Shell and Tate who are cutting a rug and looking happier than ever I guess things come together when you conquer your demons. Oh yea and about Mel; he and Destiny are expecting a little girl any day now and are a cutest little couple he also sent the last shot that killed Vee. I mean it isn't any better but my son ain't do it Soooooo. I laugh to myself as I look at my mommy and daddy Lo—man their story is epic, in my eyes they are the epitome of black love. I guess you go through hell to get to the promise land because they sure are happy. My cousin Charli is living her best life look at her over there two stepping with Supreme. Truth is making her life great she just took another offer to model for Jon Marc in Paris this year she and Sincere had a beautiful babygirl they named Alana so she dedicated two years to her and is now back in the curvy model scene and on big things. My big sisters are even enjoying themselves over there with Leo who has taken a liking to some new little thing named Cherry he has with him could be something maybe not if you ask me he keeping her around to try to make Truth jealous but she's clearly unbothered. Things are really looking better. There were a lot of uneasy truths to swallow but we made it.

"Boom!" it sounded like a bomb went off and the room got smoky.

"FBI everybody down!"

"Awww fuck! Some shit be too good to be true..."

An Uneasy Truth 2

Made in the USA
Middletown, DE
04 June 2025

76550817R00156